dark
secret love

Also by Alison Tyler

A Is for Amour

Afternoon Delight

B Is for Bondage

Best Bondage Erotica

Best Bondage Erotica, Volume 2

The Big Book of Bondage

C Is for Coeds

Caught Looking (with Rachel Kramer Bussel)

D Is for Dress-Up

Down and Dirty

E Is for Exotic

Exposed

F Is for Fetish

Frenzy

G Is for Games

Got a Minute?

H Is for Hardcore

The Happy Birthday Book of Erotica

Heat Wave

Hide and Seek (with Rachel Kramer Bussel)

Hurts So Good

I Is for Indecent

J Is for Jealousy

K Is for Kinky

L Is for Leather

Love at First Sting

Luscious

The Merry XXXmas Book of Erotica

Morning, Noon and Night

Naughty or Nice?

Never Have the Same Sex Twice

Open for Business

Playing with Fire

Pleasure Bound

Red Hot Erotica

Slave to Love

Sudden Sex

Three-Way

dark secret love

a story of submission

by ALISON TYLER

CLEiS
PRESS

Published in the United States by Cleis Press, Inc., 2246 Sixth Street, Berkeley, California 94710.

Printed in the United States.
Cover design: Scott Idleman/Blink
Cover photograph: gremlin/Getty Images
Text design: Frank Wiedemann

First Edition.
10 9 8 7 6 5 4 3 2 1

Trade paper ISBN: 978-1-57344-956-4
E-book ISBN: 978-1-57344-978-6

Introduction

Welcome to my world. Have a seat. Make yourself at home.

I'm about to tell you a story. To open my closet and expose my desires, my fantasies, my truth and my fiction—as well as my ass, clad in silky scarlet knickers. In 2006, I began this journey. "A sulphurous personal memoir of past sexual activities which put Belle de Jour's timid exploits in the shade." was how *The Guardian* described my words.

This is who I am and how I got here. I've changed the names. I've tweaked and redesigned, camouflaged and unraveled. This is meta-fiction, beta-fiction, masturbatory fiction. I'm there, but I'm hiding behind my long dark hair. I'm there, but I've got a different name. You can hear my words. You can feel my breath whispering against your neck. How much of my tale is real? As much as I was able to give.

I wish I could provide an atmosphere to accompany each chapter. I'm an excellent hostess. I'd pour you a drink. Make you comfortable on a sleek leather sofa or a leopard-print fainting couch. Light a fire, or open all the windows to let in the cool night air. Depending on the mood, you see, depending on the scene. The low lights. The scent of the candles. And the music? The Stones. The Cure. Roxy Music. Pink Floyd. Zeppelin.

I should be able to create the proper ambiance to accompany the story.

But I can't, of course, and so I'm hoping the words will suffice. I'm hoping to paint the proper picture. I want you to know the way the cold wood felt under my bare feet. I want you to be able to trace a cut-crystal whiskey glass with your fingertips, to feel the sting of a slap and see the rising blush.

Ultimately, I'm simply a girl on a quest. And what I'm trying to discover, what I'm always working to uncover, is this:

Why do I need what I need? Why do I want what I want?

I ask those questions every day.

The soul of my story is as honest as my answers can possibly be.

My past is here. My youth is here. My Doms are here—with their attitude and their dark yearning for pain.

I've got this desire right now to confess. To spill my secrets. To share my cravings. I'm driven. I'm focused. The blue-purple prints of fatigue beneath my dark brown eyes are my badges of honor. That feeling of being used swallows me up, the soreness, the ache—those sensations consume me.

As I hope my words (and my world) will consume you.

XXX,
Alison Tyler

Prologue:
Behind Blue Eyes

Some men just know.

I've been lucky enough to find those men several times in my life.

When I was eighteen, a senior in high school, I met Brock at a concert. I didn't have to tell him anything. He saw me and gave me his number scrawled on a paper napkin. Call me, was all it said. I could barely wait until dawn the next day to dial the digits.

During our first kiss (moments into our first date), he bit my bottom lip so hard that when I ran my tongue over the indents, I could feel the echo of pain—that tiny spark. There are days I swear I still feel his lips on mine. He held my glossy dark ponytail firmly in his fist when he kissed me, pulling a little too tightly, telling me in that subtle way that he was in charge.

He was spanking me regularly by that weekend.

Some men just know.

Brock would come to my high school at lunchtime and

take my panties off, sliding them into his pocket so that I was forced to spend the rest of the day bare under my skirt. He would slip me away on his Harley for twenty-minute quickies that always involved his belt, or his leather motorcycle gloves, or his open hand on my bare ass.

I'd spent my whole life being as good a girl as I possibly could, and Brock let me know it wasn't enough. I could never be good enough. I would always fail in some unforeseen way, and he would be forced to punish me.

Because he knew.

On the night of our first date, as we walked through the darkness near my house, he stopped and pressed me up against the side of a parked car. "What's your secret fantasy?" he murmured, so soft against my skin. "You can tell me, baby. You can tell me anything."

My goal, my dream, my deepest desires have always rested in taking it. Lowering my head, gritting my teeth, and bearing the pain, the humiliation. But I couldn't tell him that. I stared at him in the glow of the streetlight, and then looked down. Brock instantly tilted my face to his. "When I ask you a question," he said, his voice more stern now, "I expect a response."

A delicious chill ran through me.

I hadn't needed to say a word.

Brock understood. He was on me in a heartbeat, and he never let up.

There were days I had to wear long-sleeved shirts to cover the evidence that I'd spent part of the weekend cuffed to his bed. There were days I couldn't sit right in class, when I stared up at the board or tried to focus on the discussion but saw nothing, heard nothing.

He made me talk, eventually. I didn't get away with

coy glances, with wishful, wistful expressions. He tied me down and asked his questions, and he forced me to answer every single one.

Brock was more than a decade my senior, and he possessed a chiseled jaw and those ice-blue eyes from the famous Who song. He wouldn't even have to speak to me, simply shoot me a look, and I would lower my head in silent submission, knowing that somehow, in some unexpected way, I'd failed him.

Because he wanted me to fail.

Of course, by failing, I won. When I misbehaved for him, he made all my fantasies come true. And it wasn't long before I realized that high-school life and my world with Brock were parallel universes that didn't have anything else in common—they were running side by side on twin tracks. I felt as if I were in a dream as I walked through the quad, watching the popular kids up on the wall, the jocks out by the basketball court, the stoners behind the gym. I faked everything from eight to three, not coming alive again until Brock picked me up on his Harley. I was smart enough to do well in class simply by going through the motions. But I no longer had a desire to fit in.

I think we are all hardwired for what we crave. When I'd gone on a few miserable dates with guys my age, I would invariably offer my wrists to them. To hold. To kiss. I didn't even know why I was doing this. And the guys never figured out what I wanted. I can imagine their confusion now. What's with this chick? But Brock did. He rarely held my hand. He gripped my wrist instead, letting me know what it would feel like to be bound to his bed, to be in his power. Letting me know ahead of time, before he made that fantasy come true.

We dated for the rest of my senior year. And then I went off to college in Los Angeles, knowing deep down that in spite of my good-girl persona, I was bad to the core. And hoping like hell that someone else would see through my faux exterior and understand.

Chapter One

Extracurricular Activities

When I arrived at college, I felt like a virgin all over again. Brock was gone, and I doubted anyone could replace him. On a lark, I made out with the dorm stud the first weekend of school, but he wound up choosing a thin-lipped blonde sorority chicklet to date instead. I crushed on a black-denim-wearing artist type who managed to tie himself into my lunar cycles. He was a quiet pervert who fucked me only when I was on the rag.

To my dismay, college guys turned out to be high school guys with better access to fake IDs and beer. I had no interest in the nightly alcohol raids, the shaving cream fights, the drama. I floated around in a cloud of unspoken desires until I found my match off campus at the grocery store. Robert was thirty-four to my nineteen, and he was as kinky as Brock—but different. Brock had been tall and lean, strong but built for speed. Robert was big, studly, hugely muscled. At six-foot four, he towered over me. Undeniably handsome, he had women swarming him at the store. Every bored housewife asked him to choose her produce.

I tried to catch his eye for months, wearing special outfits to spark his interest. But it wasn't until the school year ended and I moved off campus that he took notice. I was painting my apartment—a skyline in graffiti—and I came into the store late wearing paint-splattered cutoffs, smudges of blue paint on my cheekbones and my arms, and he couldn't get enough. Here was the first man I'd ever met who liked a "sweet disorder in the dress" (if you know that Herrick poem), rather than neat and pristine. As soon as I walked into the store, he came forward. He had been in the middle of arranging fresh fruits, and while I watched, he pulled a knife from his pocket and cut open a peach. He didn't offer me the piece; he fed it to me.

Within minutes, we were fucking in the service elevator at the grocery store, and later that night he arrived at my apartment to continue our games. Like Brock, he understood me from the start. There were no romantic whisperings. No cajoling or gentle touching. He lifted me up and held me against the wall, fucking me with a brutal intensity. I'm slightly built—five-foot four in flats—and he could move me however he chose. Bending me over the sofa, carrying me to the windows, spreading me out on the dining room table. We didn't sleep until dawn. And for that whole summer, he came to my place when his shift was over, between midnight and three AM, and told me all of the things he wanted to do to me.

"I want to fuck you on top, on your side, up the ass..." His hands were huge and roamed over my body as if he'd owned me from the start. I was weak in his presence, needing him, craving his warmth. Finding safety in his size alone.

But then I went and did something unbelievably stupid—depriving me of any sexual pleasure for three lonely years.

Chapter Two:
My Mistake

My mistake's name was Byron. I met him at a party for the newspaper where I interned during my freshman year at college. I had hit the ground running after landing in Southern California, hosting a late-night radio show on the college station (I won the spot with an essay, beating out four hundred other contestants), writing for the college paper, and interning at an alternative weekly. Although I wound up despising school, I loved Los Angeles from the moment I entered Hollywood, and I lived for my job. I'd worked on the paper in high school, had been writing since I could grip a pencil, but this was my first real name-on-the-masthead gig.

My poor editor didn't know what to make of me. I was shy and quiet, but extremely proficient. I could jam out well past a hundred words a minute. At the time, there was no Internet, and staff writers either dropped off their stories on disk—big, flimsy floppy disks—or faxed them in. My main job was to key in the pieces that arrived by fax. But I also brewed coffee, made photocopies, ran errands.

That's how I met Byron. He was a former frat-boy friend of the owners who would drop by from time to time to get lunch or shoot the shit. Eventually, he stopped striding past my desk on the way to my bosses' offices and began hanging out to chat.

He was twenty-six when we met, but seemed older. He dressed in an artsy, European style and drove a crimson convertible. I asked him out once on a lark, to go to a screening with me, and he turned me down flat. He was no teacher. He didn't date teens.

I didn't pursue him heavily. I took no for an answer and continued to see Robert. Not to date him—we never went out—but to fuck him. And then came Halloween—in what would have been my sophomore year, had I been actually attending classes. The newspaper held an annual staff party in a revolving steakhouse restaurant on top of a local office building. Byron was there on a date, but he ended up flirting with me. I attended the party because I was staff, but I couldn't buy drinks. Byron kept sliding over to me with vodkas in hand, and finally steered me back to the booth. He sat me at his side, stroking my thigh under the table while his girlfriend stared daggers at me. I didn't care. I wish I could say I did, but I didn't.

It was an alcohol-drenched night, and the following day, Byron showed up at the office, pulling me aside to say, "You know, if you play with the big kids, you could get burned."

"Is that what you are?" I asked. "Big kids?"

He didn't intimidate me. I was used to Doms. He liked that I didn't back down. We started dating, though not exclusively. Byron was always quick to tell me about the other women he was dating, although I kept quiet about my own activities, seeing no need to share. I met up with Robert after dates with Byron. I knew that the chemistry was better with my midnight-to-three man, but I was confused. I thought I was supposed to end up with someone like Byron, a man with prospects, with a solid education. With a goal greater than stacking perfectly proportioned fruit pyramids.

What did I know? I was only nineteen.

Chapter Three:
Heart of Glass

Byron made it clear to me that I was not his one and only. We were still free agents, able to see (and by "see" he meant "fuck") other people without any of that nasty emotion called guilt. But I was his first choice for a date on Valentine's Day, a time for lovers—he said this in a way that let me know I'd won some sort of prize in his book. Unfortunately, Byron was fighting off a cold. He took me out for an expensive dinner downtown and gave me an intricate violet lace corset from a fancy store. And then he drove me back to his place and passed out.

"You don't have to stay," were his last words before his head hit the pillow.

I called this chapter "Heart of Glass," but I should have called it "Slut." Say the word slowly with me. Wrap your tongue around it. Stretch it out sensuously. Sss-llll-uttt.

I'd have been loyal if I'd stayed. But Byron had told me the rules of the game so many times they were tattooed on my heart: if I played with the big kids, I might get burned. And that remark left me free in my mind to bring my new present to the grocery store and wait until the end of Robert's shift. I parked right up front, and when I walked into the store, his handsome face lit up immediately.

"One minute," he said, "I have a few things to buy."

If he was surprised to see me, he didn't show any sign. He simply clocked out and walked into the parking lot, brown paper bag under one arm, bouquet in hand. Grocery store flowers—cheap and dyed and perfect.

We went to his place at the beach, nearly empty, totally nondescript. He poured champagne into jelly glasses and we toasted each other.

Slut.

Is the word echoing in your head yet? It should be. Because after downing the first glass, I excused myself from our party on the living room floor in order to use Robert's bathroom. And inside that tiny space, I slipped on my newest piece of lingerie, working those intricate pearl buttons into the holes that ran the length of the form-fitting piece. It was tiny, a 32A, an ideal fit. There was a matching lace thong that covered just about nothing. But I knew I wouldn't have either piece on for long.

Robert whistled when I came back into the room. And then he stood and lifted me into his arms and held me up against the wall. His favorite way to fuck. He was brutal by nature. Massively different from Byron. There were no books in his apartment. No pictures on the walls. He didn't really exist in the place. It was simply where he went to sleep. Like a cave. A dwelling, not a home.

But it was exactly what I wanted. The way he held

me against him, his massive chest, his rock-like body. I had one of those sweet, drunken discussions with a girl-friend the other day, and we giggled about "cocks we've known." Robert's is one of the few that I can remember in great detail. In my memories, he is always erect.

And on this night, he fucked me for hours. With me riding him, my back on the wall, legs around his waist, the lace of my thong pushed to the side. Then with me bent over the edge of his thrift-store sofa, gritting my teeth as he slammed against me. Never slowing down. Never needing to pause.

Slut.

He spanked me with those great big mitts of his. Spanked me because he liked the sound and the feel and the way I got wetter with each stroke. He knew enough to pull me over his lap, to put me in the proper pose, to hiss the statements that would take me where I needed to go.

"Bad girl, showing up after midnight to get fucked."

"Yes, Robert."

"You know what I ought to do to you, don't you?"

He was sex incarnate. And although I could tell that he loved the dainty finery of the lingerie, he couldn't be gentle with the pieces. He was always rough, needing to pull at the lace rather than waste precious time working the buttons to get the corset off. Tearing the panties with his paws, leaving the whole new outfit in tatters.

I flashed on Byron, passed out on his bed, half a world away in Hollywood, not dreaming I could be this deviant. No inkling at all that I could be this bad.

"Such a slut...Tell me what you need...Come on, girl. Say it."

I stayed all night with Robert. Or all that was left of the night. I didn't mind that it was already February 15th by the time he'd clocked out of work. Didn't mind that Cupid had left the building. I got precisely what I wanted on Valentine's Day. The perfect gift for the perfect slut.

One rainy night soon after, I found myself unexpectedly engaged in a threesome with a sultry female vocalist and her dark-haired, dark-eyed roommate, an up-and-coming soap-opera star who boasted the mournful look of a young Dean Martin. These were friends from the paper, and throughout the evening, various acquaintances wandered through our lair. Someone wanted clothing advice for a gig he was playing. Another needed to borrow cash. Despite what you might have heard, I was a willing participant. I was tipsy but not drunk. I wasn't entirely nude (at least not while others were present)—I had on Ava's gold satin robe. This wasn't my first ménage (although the previous one had been with two guys, and Playboy's advisor calls that a "gang bang" rather than a ménage à trois). The upshot is that although I never told Byron everything that happened (about how Charlie cradled my face in his hands while he fucked me, about how he crooned "Oh my girls, my sweet girls" as Ava and I took turns licking his cock clean), Byron thought he had me all figured out. Or had himself all figured out. I think he truly believed I joined in the sexfest to get him to notice me. Not true at all. You would have joined in, too.

Ava was this stunning green-eyed blonde, and I looked up to her. Eight years my senior, she seemed so worldly. Sure, she worked two other jobs while trying to further her music career, but she made everything look so easy. Effortless. She dated handsome, older men who gave her gifts, and she fucked young actors who fueled her libido. Charlie was one of them. He looked like the movie star he later became. Beside the way they looked, they wanted me. Charlie thought my naïveté was charming. He couldn't wait to demolish my inhibitions. What he and Ava—what most people, in fact—didn't understand was that I didn't have many inhibitions.

There's a difference between being shy and being pure.

Mystery is everything. The Monday after the infamous ménage, Byron arrived at the office at 8:30 and asked me what had happened. When I shrugged and said simply that I'd spent the weekend with Ava, he insisted that I move in with him. For no sane reason, I did, effectively saying goodbye to good sex and hello to nearly three years of the worst sort of submission.

The submission of the soul.

From Byron's extremely arrogant manner, from the precise way he dressed and spoke and wrote, I had believed that he would treat me in the way that my prior beaus had. But no. He was very willing to be dominant about everything but sex. While we'd dated, he had teased me with public displays of affection. Kissing me at clubs, twining his fingers in my hair when we were out at plays. All of that stopped as soon as I moved in. It was as if he only would do those sorts of things with a disposable girlfriend. Potential wives were to be treated in an entirely different manner.

Finally, in a fit of angst, I got drunk and confessed what I truly wanted. What I needed. I thought—hoped, prayed—that perhaps he was treating me with kid gloves because he was worried that he would hurt me. I couldn't have been more off base. When I got his wood-backed hairbrush and begged him on my knees to use it on me, he gave me a look of such marked disgust that I wanted to vanish into the floor. In the morning, I blamed the X-rated confession on drunkenness and we never spoke of it again.

Why did I stay? No fucking clue, except that I was younger, and dumber, and somehow under his control. When we went out to eat one night with friends, the lady in the couple let slip that I'd told her a secret about one of Byron's buddies. I hadn't known this was a secret, but when Keri turned to Byron and spoke the secret aloud, he turned to me and said, "You lost ten points."

All right, if this happened to me now, I would have gotten up and left. No question. But then, I panicked. My heart stopped. Ten points? Out of how many? How could I earn them back?

The few times I had the nerve to fight with him, he would get a smug look on his face, listen to me rant, and then respond either with "You're so pretty" or "Silly girl," as if nothing I said managed to stick in his brain. The worst thing of all was that everyone always told me how lucky I was. We made a cute couple, and feeling sure that I was the damaged one, I tried my best to be the good little girlfriend he wanted. I bought the brands of soap (Dial), laundry detergent (Tide), mouthwash (Scope), and toilet paper (Charmin) his mommy had bought. I dressed in the style he requested—pencil skirts, crisp shirts. I wore my hair the way he liked, pin-straight and in a high ponytail. I acted the part of the sub in every way, except sexually.

Until I snapped.

When I asked him why we rarely had sex, he polled his brothers and father to determine whether we were on average with the rest of the men in his family. When I showed him books of erotica that indicated I wasn't wicked for wanting more, he said he thought of me like a sister.

Unfortunately, I didn't break up well. I flamed out. With his diamond ring sparkling on my finger, I engaged in several devious yet delicious affairs. I'm no cheat at heart. But when I was honest with him and told him I needed to try life on my own, he demanded I seek professional help. He wouldn't hear a word I had to say. ("You're so pretty.") I felt that there was nowhere else for me to go. Nowhere except into the cherry-red convertible of a handsome young man named Connor.

Chapter Four:
How I Became a Meat Eater

Almost everyone in Los Angeles is a something-slash-something-else. A waiter/underwear model. A comedian/traffic school instructor. An actress/dog walker. Connor was a model/bartender who worked in a restaurant at an upscale office building in Beverly Hills. Of the four bartenders at this restaurant, one was a bartender/musician, one a bartender/actor, and one a bartender/model. Only one was a bartender/bartender.

The building was where Byron and I both worked. Byron played the role of right-hand man to a flamboyant gay screenwriter, and he got me a part-time slot as the screenwriter's personal assistant. Yeah, there's a difference. Byron listened to Jody read his dialogue aloud for hours at a time. I organized Jody's closets, booked his salon appointments, and kept his day planner (to make sure his boyfriend never found out about his lovers on the side). The job was mindless and I enjoyed working in the beautiful building, but I hated my life.

Every time I drove my car under an underpass, I'd have fantasies about turning the wheel sharply into the concrete wall. During my forty-minute commute from the beach to Beverly Hills, I played Bowie incessantly—Ashes to Ashes, We Could Be Heroes, John, I'm Only Dancing—and cried for no reason at all. Although I told the people I most trusted that I was unhappy—my family, my friends—nobody believed me. Every single person told me that I was simply young (true) and had cold feet (false) about my impending wedding. I wanted to escape, but I didn't know how.

This was such a dark time that I don't really remember a lot about it. I don't even remember all that much about Byron, except for my constant "point" losses and his continual critiques. From the mundane to the extreme, he didn't like it when I:

wore my hair curly
wore my glasses
wore miniskirts
wore pants without pockets
drank beer
read trashy magazines.

I'd been a vegetarian the whole time we were together, and although he was a carnivore, he would not hear of me deciding to eat meat again. He didn't like my tattoos, didn't like it when I dyed my brown hair black, didn't like the short stories I wrote. He was anal about everything but sex. That's not true—he was anal about sex, too, but not into anything back-door or kinky. Sex had to happen in a specific lights-out, minty-fresh sort of way. The longer we were together, the less frequently and more lifelessly we made love.

We never, ever fucked.

Yet, although I seemed unable to please him, he didn't want me to change in any way.

When he was upset with me, which was often, he would refuse to speak, to acknowledge my presence at all. On the day of our engagement party, he was angry with me for some inconsequential error. Byron didn't say a word to me all evening, didn't look at me once until he gave a toast to his future bride, a toast that actually brought tears to people's eyes as he professed this great well of love he had for me.

Crazy. I thought I was going crazy.

"See?" my friends said. "He's lovely. Listen to how he gushes about you. I wish I had a boyfriend like that." They didn't know that he didn't speak to me for three days after the party. Didn't know that he would simply grunt if I was in his path. He had other cruel ways of punishing me: ridiculing me in front of his friends and so on. But the silent treatment was the worst. I'd grovel, trying to figure out how to make him happy, ultimately feeling like a failure twenty-four hours a day.

I'm not trying to justify why I cheated. I'm only telling my side of the story. Unlike Byron, Connor appeared to adore everything about me (including my cigarette pants with no pockets—which he said made my ass look amazing—and my newly dyed black hair, which he thought was gothic, like Bettie Page). He started by sticking little Post-It notes on my windshield. "You look beautiful," he'd write. Or "God, you're so damn sexy." I didn't believe him right away. Byron never told me I was beautiful. (His evil "You're so pretty" doesn't count.) If I asked him how I looked before an evening out, he said I was fishing for compliments, which in his view was a major sin. I stared in the mirror and saw the wrong hair, the wrong glasses, the wrong makeup, the wrong everything.

Connor saw something else.

He asked me out on a date, knowing my situation but not worrying about it. We met up for a movie in Century City and sat next to each other. We were both careful not to touch one another, yet accidentally, his arm brushed mine, my leg brushed his. Flickers of electricity flared through me. The tiniest touch was enough to make me shift in my seat, immediately aroused. I saw not one frame of that film.

Over beers afterwards, we played that same game, his foot touching mine under the table, mine brushing his, until finally, on the cusp of exploding, we retreated to the parking garage and made out like long-lost lovers. Connor couldn't keep his hands off me. He cradled my face in his strong hands, kissed me so firmly. He didn't touch me too forcefully, didn't want to leave marks that I wouldn't have been able to explain, but I felt from that first moment that I was his.

After that, it was all over. Every day we met up somewhere at the office building, on the loading deck in back, in the kitchen of the restaurant, in his car, in the parking garage. Every free second, we found a way to meet. I remember standing in front of him on the loading dock. He had on black jeans and a white T-shirt and leaned against the concrete wall of the building, looking at me. I ran my hand down his flat stomach to the crotch of his jeans, could feel how much he wanted me. He tilted his head up and closed his eyes and let me stroke him. "You're gonna make me come if you keep that up," he said, his voice harsh.

"I know," I promised him. "I know."

I felt as if I were on fire all the time, and suddenly Byron's critiques began to roll off me. I found that I didn't care much if he wasn't talking to me. Silence was better than constant nagging, than losing another ten fucking points. I didn't care if he hated my outfits. I was no longer looking for his approval. I was no longer dressing for him.

My newfound glow brought comments from elsewhere. Alain, at the upscale market. Johnny, an actor I ran into now and then in Santa Monica. Hunter, my former editor. People noticed a marked difference in me—at least, everyone did but Byron. I took great pleasure in the fact that Byron hated Connor, that he called him dumb, clearly intimidated because Connor was so handsome—and this is the funny thing. I've never been into handsome. I'm much more of a Billy Bob Thornton than a Brad Pitt sort of girl. But Connor was a modern James Dean, blonde and blue-eyed and almost angelic, the kind of stunning that turns heads. I didn't want him for those reasons. I craved him because he saw something in me, even at my most beaten down, and he went after me. I have a photo of him following a night of no sleep. He's wearing black jeans and no shirt under an open blazer, and he's smoking a cigarette, but barely, the butt dangling from his lower lip. He has that insolent fuck you look that has always made me wet in a heartbeat.

The longer we were together, the bolder I became. I found ways to avoid sleeping in Byron's bed. I'd stay up late, watching reruns on TV and drinking tequila, which I hid in the cupboard behind the unused vinegar, because although Byron drank and smoked pot daily, he didn't like it when I was tipsy. I made sure that Byron was fast asleep before I curled up on the sofa and made myself come, thinking about Connor, picturing his body on mine, his mouth on the curve of my neck, his hands holding me in place, never letting me go. I envisioned him doing the things to me that Robert had, that Brock had. I envisioned him fucking me, cuffing me, binding me in place. And when I told him my darkest secrets, he didn't run away. He didn't look at me with pity as if I were demented or broken. He simply said, "I know, Samantha. I know what you want." A dark laugh. "I knew from the first time I saw you."

Connor wrote me sexy letters. He called and talked dirty to me when I was in the office, feet away from Byron. He brought me trinkets, a leather cuff-style bracelet that I wore every day. One afternoon he confessed his own fantasy, in which we went to the Sunset Strip tattoo parlor and he watched as the man tattooed a design on me that Connor had drawn himself. He wanted to own me, to mark me, and I felt as if I were melting as he confessed each frame.

We went to Melrose early one evening, when I was supposed to be running an errand for Jody, and I got my ear double-pierced, sitting on Connor's lap while the clerk did his job. I felt Connor's cock stiffen in his black jeans. Christ, we were well suited for one another, our fantasies melding. The only thing working against us was time. There never was enough.

I look back and wonder why in the hell Byron insisted that we move forward with the wedding. He must have known how unhappy I was with him. And he seemed to hate me. Really hate me. Someone who loves you doesn't put you down all the time. He claimed he was trying to help me, to better me, to teach me. Yet that was one of the first things he had told me when we'd met: I'm not a teacher. Prior to me, he had dated only older women, sophisticated type As. And here I was, an out-of-control filly, needing a strong hand, a firm set of reins.

Whenever we fought and I'd pack to leave, he'd insist I would regret it for the rest of my life. "And where will you go, silly girl?" he asked, taunting me, because I lived in a house he owned, worked at a job he'd gotten me. He assured me I'd be homeless, jobless, penniless. So I stayed, physically, but mentally I was already far away. I wore my pants without pockets. I wore my glasses when I wanted to. And I became a meat eater.

Oh, yes, I did.

Connor and I met for lunch at a steakhouse, and I remember the pleasure of cutting into the rare flesh, of eating bite after bite. Of him feeding me from his plate. Nothing has ever tasted that good.

Chapter Five:
Changing to Chanel

I returned from a tryst with Connor to find Byron livid, ready to confront me. Someone had spilled our secret. I don't think I said a word. I had no defense. When Byron and I parted, he took all of the keys from my ring save my car key: the two house keys, garage key, two office keys, key to his parents' house. Since he'd worked for Jody longer than I had, he easily had me fired. Almost all of our friends were his friends. I remember feeling free but terrified. When he asked me for his ring back, I gave him the ultimate fuck-you—pulling it from my red leather change purse rather than off my finger.

He called me a cunt, and I suppose I deserved it. I had become such a remnant of my former self that I was practically unrecognizable. At twenty-two I had been cleanly transformed into a robotic Stepford wife ("Must buy Dial. Must buy Tide. Must buy Charmin.") But I knew what I wanted—I didn't need a man with positive future prospects or a rich daddy. I needed what I'd had in high school, someone who could look at me and see who I really was. Someone who wouldn't laugh or scowl or turn away in disgust when I confessed my darkest fantasies.

Someone who had a brush and a belt and a set of cuffs and was not afraid to use them.

As I was walking out of the office, my solitary key in hand, Byron called out for me to stop. I turned around to face him, wondering what he might possibly have to follow up calling me a cunt. It still brings a smile to my face to remember that he spat out: "Los Angeles isn't big enough for the both of us." I don't know what part he thought he was playing. I do know he didn't hold much stock in my ability to survive on my own. Maybe he was right, because my first instinct wasn't to try to line up housing or call my friends, or even have a drink.

The first thing I did after leaving Byron was head to the mall.

Perhaps I ought to have been better prepared for our inevitable parting, but when we finally broke up, we were at work. When Byron took away my keys, I had no way to get back into our house to pick up my belongings. My parents lived eight hundred miles away. Most of my friends were Byron's friends, who I was sure would not see me in a very positive light.

One of Byron's many quaint little quirks was his insane insistence that I never change my perfume. I'd been wearing Anaïs Anaïs since I was twelve, and as far as he was concerned, I was going to wear that sickly-sweet scent until I died. So after running through the whole slew of perfumes at the Macy's counter, I wound up with a classic bottle of Chanel #5. (And since that day, I have been extremely fickle. I've never managed to choose another signature scent.) I also bought several bras and knickers and a silky little golden nightgown before crossing the street to Rexall for toiletries—and no, I didn't buy Dial or Scope or Crest or any of the mandatory items on Byron's persnickety shopping list. I could break the rules for once—Colgate and Listerine and Chanel, oh my! Luckily, I did have clothes. Byron always hated my constant refusal to pick up my dry cleaning on time. When we broke up, I was able to collect several of my favorite dresses from the cleaners—my procrastination paying off.

I headed to a French hotel I'd always admired and booked a room. I had almost no money, but I had plastic. Connor came to stay that night—of course he did—and for the first time since we'd begun flirting months before, we had time.

Everything we'd done together so far had been shadowed by the need to rush, to look over our shoulders, to watch our backs. Now Connor could work slowly. He didn't say a word after I let him into the room, simply backed me up until I felt the bed against my legs. I sat on the edge of the heavy brocade comforter, then slid away from him toward the plush pillows, unsure from the look on his face of what he wanted me to do, what he expected me to say. Connor wasn't unsure at all. He stared at me with his head cocked to the side while he slowly pulled his belt from the loops of his jeans. My heart went crazy. I couldn't stare directly at him, yet I knew better than to look away. I sat up on the bed with my feet curled under me, shifting my hips while I waited for him to speak. Flashes of what we'd done so far played like movie clips in my mind: the way he'd held me against the wall while he kissed me. The way he'd taken my panties down, inch by inch, then slipped them into his pocket, forcing me to go bare, like Brock had. The way he always let up on me before leaving a mark, knowing I had to go home at some point. Knowing other eyes would see me.

Nobody was going to see me now. Only Connor.

"Roll over, Sam," he said, that husky rawness to his voice. "You know what to do."

I did know. I'd been sliding my fingers between my thighs late every night for months now, knowing. I'd had vibrant, Technicolor dreams where I'd wake up with my hands trapped under me, thinking I was bound to Connor's bed before realizing I had simply bound myself in my fantasies.

"Come on, Sam, don't make me wait."

There was power in the way he spoke. I tend to choose older men, always going for experience over youth. But Connor was somewhat of a prodigy. Only twenty-five but with a dominant side already well tuned and finely polished.

"I've waited long enough—"

He was right, yet I was frozen, mesmerized by the look of his worn belt in his hands, by the glinting light in the room, by the sounds of the traffic outside. I thought of that time in the movie theater, when we had worked not to touch one another. I thought of making him come outside, against the wall of the building, my hand stroking the faded denim of his jeans. I thought of Byron and the look of disgust on his face after our night out partying, when I'd drunk vodka straight from the bottle and then humiliated myself by begging him to spank me with his hairbrush. Was that why I'd stayed with him for so fucking long? Because he owned that image of me and I'd been desperate to erase it, to prove that I wasn't broken after all?

Connor didn't say another word, didn't give me

another chance—he moved with feline grace, grabbing me and pulling me over his lap into a slightly altered position from the one he'd initially requested. I lowered my head, tears of shame already stinging my eyes. Not because he was going to punish me over his lap, but because I'd already failed him, failed to follow a simple command. He dropped the belt and started with his hand, smacking his palm against the semi-sheer fabric of my brand-new nightie. I held myself as still as possible, emotion flooding through me, trying to behave for Connor as I'd tried for Byron. I'd made Byron my Dom. He hadn't given me anything I wanted, but I had supplicated myself for him, suffocated myself for him, hoping perhaps somewhere in the deep recesses of my brain that he'd ultimately reward me if I was good enough.

Hadn't I learned anything from Brock? With the right man in charge, I would never be good enough. That was the whole point. Connor taught me that little lesson again, his strong hand carefully slipping the golden fabric to my hips, then dragging my panties down my thighs. He used his open palm again and again, and soon thoughts stopped as the flush of pain took over. Still I didn't struggle. I didn't make a sound. Which told Connor quickly enough that he had to work me more seriously. He didn't want my silence. He wanted to know that the spanking was having a proper effect. Only when my skin was cherry-flushed to his satisfaction did he push me back onto the bed and tell me to lock my hands together over my head. I licked my bottom lip, then bit into it as I saw him double his belt before making the leather snap.

I felt as if I'd been underwater for three years. Felt as if for the first time in ages, I could finally breathe. Connor set his hand against my cheek. He bent down and kissed me, and then stood back and let the belt meet my ass for the first time. The sound of the belt was more intense than the first stripe. That whip-crack of leather through silence, then the intake of my breath, and Connor admonished me, "Stay still, Sam. Don't move. Don't move an inch. You've got a long fucking night ahead of you. And you know it, too. Because you deserve this. Don'tcha? Don't you deserve this?" It was a crooning question, almost singsong, making fun of me somehow, teasing me.

When I didn't speak right away, he was on me as Brock had been. Always answer a direct question. Don't forget this. Learn from my mistakes. His hand tilting my chin up towards him, his eyes flashing a look I'd never seen in their striking blue before.

And suddenly I understood. He wasn't punishing me because I wanted it, because I touched myself at night and dreamed of him being rough with me. He was doing this because for four months I had flirted with him, had kissed him, had fucked him, and then gone back home to someone else. He had never asked me to leave Byron, had rarely mentioned the man's name at all. But he had known that I kept my clothes lined up neatly next to Byron's in the closet. That I ate breakfast each morning at his table, when I could stomach a bite. That I spent weekends with his family.

I hadn't been unfaithful to Byron. I had cheated on Connor.

The belt flashed in the air, and I gritted my teeth and told myself that I would take whatever he had to give. I owed him. Sure, I had almost zero money in the bank. But that didn't matter to Connor. That night he made me pay with something far more precious than cash.

Chapter Six:
Black Coffee in Bed

In the morning, Connor had to get up at five for a photo shoot. We'd had a ferocious night fucking, and I remember looking up at him, bleary-eyed, as he gave me his classic smirk and pulled on his boots. I ordered room-service coffee and stared out the window, watching Los Angeles wake up and realizing I'd never have to worry about whether I'd bought the proper mouthwash again.

Goodbye, Byron.

When I rolled over on the mattress, I saw that Connor had left his belt hanging over the back of the chair. My stomach tightened and I closed my eyes, picturing the previous evening, imagining what might happen to me on the next. I simply had to wait sixteen hours or so until we could be together again. After the modeling gig, Connor had to work at the restaurant. And where did I have to be? Nowhere. The whole time I was with Byron, I went to school part-time and worked part-time. Over the three years, I had worked at the newspaper, at a clothes store, as a personal assistant, at a magazine, at a movie theater, and as a masseuse.

Recently, I had been splitting my time between the screenwriter's office and the home of a fairly well-known movie star. But I'd been let go from the movie star's house because I had worn a diaphanous dress around her director husband, who apparently hadn't been vaccinated against girls in sheer sundresses.

"Diaphanous" was her word. It was simply a sundress, one of my favorites, pale pink with tiny pearl buttons down the front. The dress wasn't tight, or even all that short, and I wore a slip beneath and stockings, yet had managed to catch the husband's eye regardless.

Now I had no job, and I desperately needed to find housing that was less costly than $240 a night. Connor called from work with the happy news that I could stay with a friend of his named Lois. She had two male roommates (don't look at me like that!) and she was happy to put me up. Connor lived with a whole slew of guys out at the beach and they had a rule against moving females into the house. (Girls in the house were considered bad luck, same as on a ship.)

I spent the morning at a café perusing the help-wanted ads, trying to figure out what I was good at. Byron hadn't thought I was good enough to do much of anything. He liked to taunt me and say that within three years, we'd have a station wagon with three kids in the back. According to Byron, I was good enough to be a wife and mom. End of story. Every time I heard his voice berating me, I closed my eyes, searching for a mental "erase" button. Free from his critiques, I answered every ad I was remotely qualified for. I spent my days driving all over the city and my nights with Connor. Everywhere with Connor.

We were back to searching for outdoor locations, for privacy in a very public city. His Venice pad was bus-stop busy with twelve guys and no place to hide. Lois and her roommates were cool, but I couldn't see paying them back for their kindness by fucking all over their apartment.

So Connor and I got creative. We used the back seat of his car, a huge cherry-red '67 Chevy. We found alleys. We fucked in Griffith Park. We went all the way in a department-store dressing room—I'd needed to buy more clothes: jeans, T-shirts, underwear. We had no fear any longer. Who the fuck cared if someone saw us? Exhibitionism has always been one of my weaknesses. Connor was more than ready to play. He wrapped my wrists with his wallet chain and spread me out in the Chevy's huge rear seat. He always took his time, looking at me, making me feel even more naked by the way he evaluated every part of my body. His hands roamed over my shoulders, my small breasts, down to the basin of my belly. He liked to hook his fingers into my nether lips and spread me wide, blowing a puff of air over my pussy before locking his lips on my clit and sucking. Making me come was no challenge for him. I melted at the way he touched me— sometimes so rough I was shaking. Sometimes so softly I'd beg him to stop teasing.

"Please—"

He loved to hear me beg.

"Please what, Sam?"

"Oh, god, Connor. You know."

"Say it."

Cruel, he was. I'd been rebuked. I'd been put down. I hated spelling out what I wanted. And Connor loved every torturous minute.

"I want to hear you say the words." His fingers traced

lightly over my ribs, making me squirm and pull away laughing. As soon as I moved away he'd be on me, biting my bottom lip, holding me in place with his body, still fully clothed. His voice whiskey-soft and dark: "Tell me. Tell me what you need."

My eyes down, my hair falling forward, unable to look at him, even though I knew he already knew. Even though I knew he didn't think I was broken, he didn't think I was damaged goods. "Spank me, Connor."

And he'd flip me over his lap and give my ass the lightest little patty-cake spanking. "Like this?"

I'd know better than to laugh, because all hell would break loose if I didn't take him seriously. I'd know to turn my head to stare up at him over my shoulder, to meet his eyes and say, "No, Connor," my voice a whisper. "Please, Connor. Spank me for real."

And, Christ, I would feel his cock grow even harder as he'd hold me in place, getting ready for the first part of the evening's punishment.

Sometimes he bent me over the hood of his car and striped me with his belt, taking the worn leather off my own waist first, his hands so rough, undoing the buckle, sliding the old brown leather free. Sometimes he talked to me while we fucked, his mouth pressed to my ear, saying the things he knew about me, things I tried to hide from the world. "Such a sweet girl," he'd say, "That's what everyone thinks. Right? But I could tell. From the way you walked. From the way you looked at me under those dark lashes, stared at me while you drank your gin."

I always wondered how he had known. Can Doms sniff out a sub at twenty feet, like police dogs smelling for drugs? L.A. is a playground for the world's most beautiful women. And Connor chose me. That's how I felt when he took me out to Griffith Park, pushed me firmly against a tree, and whipped me before taking my ass.

He chose me.

It made the job search less painful. It made the fact that Byron still would not let me into the house to collect my belongings more bearable. Connor made me whole. I was used to sleeping alone on a sofa, so that part of the equation didn't matter. Lois and her two roommates actually spoke to me, which created a far friendlier environment than the silent treatment my world had become at home.

And then Connor arrived at Lois's early one evening with the announcement that Byron had gotten him fired from the bar. (Jody was part owner of the building, and he had pull.) Connor was more than a bartender. He was a model. But the lack of a steady check was enough to make him reevaluate his world. Now, he told me, he'd had enough of L.A., and he was moving back home to Georgia. Did I want to go with him?

Georgia.

I looked out the window, at the fading light turning the bougainvillea a gold-tipped violet. I looked at Connor, with his blonde hair falling into his face, his clear blue eyes, his "I'm gonna fuck you in two minutes" expression. And I shook my head.

Chapter Seven:
Goodbye and Good Luck

"Be ready for me," Connor said over the phone. "I'll be over in ten."

"Ready?" my voice trailed upward, making a question of the single word, while my mind raced. Ready. I already knew what that meant. Connor had considered our last two weeks together as a sort of sexual boot camp. He spent his days packing boxes of belongings to ship home, saying goodbye to friends, tying up loose ends.

He spent his nights tying up loose ends, too. Pulling the ends of loose scarves until they tightened securely around my wrists. Fastening a blindfold over my eyes, capturing my ankles with his leather belt. He was determined to educate me, to make my fantasies come true. We took our opportunities wherever we could find them. This was our last weekend together, and we finally had a true place to play. All three roommates were gone until Monday—Lois to Santa Barbara, Nathan to Vegas, Garrett to San Francisco.

Connor and I had the place to ourselves.

The night before, he'd surprised me with a bag of supplies from a local sex toy store: a red-and-black paddle, a soft purple suede flogger, a set of silver cuffs. And there were more gifts, ones he didn't let me open yet. He hadn't used any on me. But he'd watched as I'd unwrapped each new toy, and when I looked up at him, he cocked a blond eyebrow at me and said, "Tomorrow night, you won't have to be quiet."

I knew what that meant. I was always quiet. Practically silent. Connor had been trying to get me to open up, to feel comfortable enough to let loose. The most I'd managed so far was a husky moan. I'd never been a screamer. I internalized everything. Tears might streak my cheeks, but I would not cry out. I could not. Connor had plans to change that.

While I waited for him, I paced the apartment, clad in an outfit we'd bought together: a short black-and-white plaid skirt, silky black T-shirt, fishnet stockings, knee-high Docs. I walked into Lois's room, where I'd set out all the toys Connor had given me. Then I paced again. He'd used his belt on me, but never a paddle. I stroked the flat side, tentatively touched the wooden handle. It was in my thoughts to try the thing on myself, to see what the pain would feel like, when I heard Connor knock.

Feeling guilty for no reason, I hurried to the front door and let him in. He had flowers with him. And a crop.

Jesus.

He looked me over, head to toe, then nodded his approval. The flowers were left to die a slow death on the cracked blue Formica kitchen counter. There wasn't even time for filling a wine bottle with water. Connor grabbed my wrist and led me back to Lois's room, a girly

37

boudoir with pink walls and a brass bed. She had angels on her dresser and her nightstand, and they looked odd as background to the various sex toys. Gargoyles would have made more sense.

Connor sat on the edge of the bed and looked at me. I knew what to do. I understood his expressions by now, could practically read his thoughts, but the crop kept me from coming forward. The way it leaned against the dresser made me want to run and hide. Not because I didn't want to feel the sting, but because I did—and that scared me to death. I'd confessed all of my secrets to Connor over our months together. I'd told him every little fucked-up fantasy I'd ever had. I couldn't hide from my truth, but I had a difficult time facing the reality head-on. Be careful what you wish for.

"Get the paddle," he said. My legs threatened to give out as I walked to the nightstand and gripped the new toy. "Over my legs, girl. Now."

I bent myself into the proper position, felt his warm hand lifting my tiny skirt, felt him watching me. He pressed the paddle against my panty-clad ass, letting me feel the weight before he landed the first blow. I sucked in my breath, but remained silent. The sting was different from the belt, but not worse. He began spanking me more rapidly, pausing only to pull my black satin bikinis down my thighs, leaving them on me, but baring my ass. The pain intensified immediately, and tears wet my eyes, but I still didn't cry out. I wasn't trying to test him. This wasn't a game. I didn't know how to do what he wanted. Not without sounding phony. Not without being fake.

"What did you think about today?" he asked, taking a break to pull my panties off completely and then herd me to the full-length mirror on the back of Lois's door, to show me my scarlet rear cheeks. He held my skirt up for me, so I could see, and he grinned at his handiwork, clearly pleased.

"This," I said. I'd gotten a temp job in an office on Wilshire, and my day had been busy, but every time I'd had a breather, I'd thought of Connor and his bag of toys.

"And this?" he queried, cupping my bare pussy with his hand and giving me a stern look, no sign of a smile now.

I wanted to melt into nothing. Disappear into a silver mist. Over one midnight confession, I'd asked him if he'd spank me...and then, unable to actually voice the request, I had simply put his hand over the front of my panties. "Spank me here...?"

For some inexplicable reason, I was always waiting for the moment when I'd go too far. When he'd give me the disgusted look that Byron had shot me after my drunken night of spilling secrets. I didn't realize that Connor's own fantasies were darker than my own, went farther than I'd dare to dream.

He'd laughed, not mean, not cruel, but still, he'd laughed at me. As if it went without saying that he'd do what I asked. "Sam," he said softly, "I have no problem punishing your pussy."

Ah, fuck me—

He carried me back to the bed, spread me out, and tied me to Lois's bed frame like the bondage pro he was. He cut my skirt off, cut my T-shirt away, undid my boots and pulled them off, then ran his fingertips over the shaved skin of my pussy. I had only my thigh-high fishnets on now. Nothing to protect me.

"You know you're a bad girl," he said, "don't you?"

I nodded, then immediately whispered, "Yes, Connor."

"And you know tonight I'm going to make you scream."

Tears started running down my cheeks, but I managed to say, "Yes, Connor."

He reached for the violet suede flogger and then he looked at me fiercely and said, "And you know you need this."

I did. I knew it. I'd known it for years.

"Tell me why."

I pleaded with my eyes. I couldn't. I didn't know.

"Try."

"Because—" was all I could say. "Because."

The flogger was light, a gentle caress at first. And then the weapon began to sting, the many tails landing faster on my tender skin. I closed my eyes and clenched my fists. But it wasn't until Connor dropped that soft, sweet toy, replacing it with the very lip of his leather belt, again and again on my pussy, putting power behind the blows, that I started to give him what he wanted. I could hear the wetness as the leather connected, and I could feel the lake of juices under my ass, and I started to cry for real.

"Open your eyes," Connor insisted.

My eyelids fluttered, and he doubled the belt and landed a blow on my upper thighs that made me gasp.

"Don't test me, girl," he said, not a faux threat. "You obey when I give a command."

He did what he said. He punished me between my legs until I came, crying out so loudly, repeating his name over and over like a mantra, knowing that it didn't matter if he was leaving. Tonight, I was his.

I mentioned that snapshot I have of Connor: black jeans, no shirt, after a night of no sleep. I took the picture myself.

I think we spent nearly forty-eight hours in bed, but that photo is from a two-AM run for coffee, the two of us sex-drenched and half naked as he headed to the closest drive-through. I had his shirt on. That's why his chest was bare. His shirt and my boots, and nothing else. He has that picture of me.

At some point during the weekend, he introduced me to the crop, and the weapon was as mean and frightening as I'd thought it would be. Later still, he grabbed clothespins from the bathroom where Lois used them to fasten her stockings to the twine strung across the shower. Connor had completely different uses for them. Oh, Christ, did he. I was humble and quiet when we were out of bed, as loud as he wanted me to be when we were on that queen-sized mattress. He'd broken that inhibition of mine, demolished my reservations to nothing.

On Sunday night, his last night in town, Connor took me up to the Sunset Strip Tattoo parlor and explained to the man behind the counter exactly what he wanted. As if he were the proprietor, Connor led me to the back room and lowered my jeans, and I dropped my chin to my chest, mortified, not only because Connor was baring my ass to strangers but because I sported bruises from when his silver buckle had caught my skin, magenta stripes from his belt, those fine thin welts from his crop. On a fair space of skin on my right hip (had Connor intentionally left that patch alone?), the tattoo artist transferred the cherries that Connor had chosen for me. Connor held my hands in his, and I looked into his eyes and stayed totally still. This was not my first tattoo, but it was the first one given to me.

"I can tell she's a naughty girl," the man said casually,

as we got ready to leave. "But keep that bandage on for at least two hours, and then rub lotion in."

We fucked one last time on Lois's bed that night. We fucked until dawn, when Connor took off the bandage and touched me so softly, so tenderly, that it made me shake more powerfully than anything else we'd done. I'd taken pain for him. I'd been marked for him. I'd done everything I set out to do.

I'm pathetic at goodbyes. Connor packed up his Chevy as the first golden light hit Hollywood. I remember the scent of the morning dew on the concrete sidewalk, the chill in the air as he gave me one final kiss...and his leather belt.

As I watched him drive away, tears streaked my face.

Should I have gone?

I don't know.

We didn't have love. We had lust. And lust is enough for midnight fuck sessions and X-rated fairy-tale fantasies, but it wasn't enough for me to move to Georgia. I slid his belt through the loops of my jeans and headed back into the triplex.

Suddenly, I was living in a world of strangers.

Chapter Eight:
She's Come Undone

You want me to have mourned him, don't you? You want me to say that I slaved long hours to save up enough money so I could go meet him, that we set up house in Georgia. It would be a dream come true, right? Connor bartending to pay the bills while I set up a typewriter on the kitchen table and pounded out porn.

But it wasn't like that. Yes, I sported a spanking-new cherry tattoo on my hip. Yes, I had Connor's belt, and I wore it whenever I had on jeans, stroking the old silver buckle absentmindedly the way he had. And yes, it took a few weeks for the bruises he left me to totally fade away.

Unfortunately, that doesn't make what we had love. And in any case, I didn't have a second to mourn. I was working as many temp jobs as I could land, shuttling all over the city wearing the few dresses I'd scavenged from the dry cleaners, trying my best to look professional. Trying to pretend I had my shit together. Weeks had passed and I still hadn't been able to get into my house and collect my stuff.

My new roommates were extremely supportive, going so far as offering to beat Byron up for me to make him return my belongings. Lois roomed with a grad student and a director, two completely different types of guys, in an old triplex in the Hollywood Hills. Nathan, the director, had dark hair, dark eyes, and a look that was insolent and sexy, in-your-face and sly. Garrett, the student, was six-foot four, barrel-chested, with choirboy good looks, and he'd recently had his heart destroyed by the heels of his college sweetheart. He seemed to be in a constant daze.

The house was surrounded by vibrant bougainvillea vines and had an old-world charm, a remnant of forties Hollywood. The interior was something else, seventies green shag carpet in the living room, cracked linoleum on the kitchen floor, stained Formica counters. Nathan and Garrett were the type of guys who stole stacks of cocktail napkins to keep by the commode rather than the pristine rolls of Charmin I was accustomed to.

I'd never had roommates like this, and I was fascinated. Odd that total strangers put me up, willingly let me sleep on their thrift-store sofa, drink their coffee, stake out their phone for interview appointments. I made their place cleaner, definitely, and more livable. I replaced the Spider-Man napkins with real toilet paper. I washed the dishes in the sink. I was suited to taking care of people. Besides, I wanted them to like me.

Although they were all friendly, Nathan intimidated the hell out of me. He had ties on the four corners of his mattress and a hidden hook behind his bed to hang hand-cuffs, which he proudly showed me on my second day in the apartment. His bookshelf boasted my favorite filthy titles: *The Story of O, Justine, The Pearl, 100 Days of Sodom.* He would come in after dates and collapse next to me on the sofa, making it feel natural to be in his arms as he told me about his X-rated adventures.

"I ate her soul," he said one night.

"You what?"

He explained that his date hadn't wanted to do something he'd requested—he left whatever that thing was to my vibrant imagination. (Anal sex? Some power game? Outdoor fucking?) And he pushed until her boundaries were broken, and then left, satisfied, while she cried. He dated extremely pretty girls, starlets he met at casting calls or out at clubs. He fucked them once and moved on. But he liked to talk to me, to stroke my dark hair away from my face and tell me his secrets. "We're exactly alike," he whispered one night to me, while I shook my head. "Don't deny it," he said, "we're two of a kind." I didn't know what he meant, and I wasn't sure I wanted to find out. But still, I liked him. I appreciated his twisted sense of humor, and I liked how confident he was.

The third roommate, Garrett, didn't pay me much attention. He seemed bemused to find me on the sofa when he came in to watch the news. He was wary of me, but friendly in a standoffish way.

This was my new life, and I did my best to be cheerful about it. I no longer had a real home, or a real room, or any real friends (mine were scattered around the country). I put my head down and worked toward getting a job. At night I wrote stories on Lois's old typewriter, deciding that if I didn't have to worry about Bryon's critiques, I might actually be able to create something worthwhile. I was plotting something—my new life. The life I'd always wanted.

* * *

Following an interview at a salon one morning, I was nearly crushed by a dog that escaped from its leash. The owner apologized profusely as he pulled the beast off me. "Really, I'm sorry," he said, and then smiled, "but if it's any consolation, he only knocks over the pretty girls."

The man invited me to dinner that night at a gourmet hotspot on Robertson to make up for the behavior of his out-of-control mutt. I hadn't been on a date-date in years. Connor and I didn't date. I was intrigued. Jack was older than me—no big surprise there, huh?—and he looked refined, like a businessman. I was excited to go out, but I met him at the restaurant, wanting to have an escape plan.

Dinner was surreal.

Jack ordered us shots and beers, strange drinks for such a fancy environment. I got drunk as my date described in minute detail what he wanted to do to me. He described the most extreme bondage, punishment, discipline. He wanted to strip me naked and make me crawl across the floor to him, to bow at his feet, to call him Sir. He wanted me to kiss the tips of his shoes, to kiss the tip of his crop, to take the pain he had in store for me.

"You need it," he said, "Don't tell me I'm wrong."

Once again, someone had found me. Snap your fingers. Strike the match. I wanted the things he described, but even drunk, I knew better than to go home with a total stranger, to let him tie me to his bed. He promised things that were constantly in my head. He said, "I know you want this. I know what you deserve."

I looked at my plate, then up at him.

"How? How do you know?"

And he laughed, like Connor had laughed. "It's clear.

46

You wear your desires on your sleeve. The longing. Almost desperate."

His hands were on me even at the table, touching me, stroking me. He cradled my face in his grip and he said, "You need it to hurt." The words were simple. Matter-of-fact. As if he'd said that my eyes were brown. Or that my skin was pale. *You need it to hurt.*

Fuck me. Why did he know? How could he tell? I took another drink, felt as if I were actually transparent, made of glass. Could everyone in the fancy restaurant see what Jack saw?

He shrugged, reading my mind so easily. "I don't know why, baby doll. I can't tell you the reasons. I can only tell you what you need." He touched my face again. "That's not totally true. I can tell you what I need as well." And he continued to talk, about the clamps he would use on my nipples and on my pussy lips, about the whips he had, about the canes. I don't think I ate more than two bites, and when he paid, he took me outside while we waited for his car. He held me in his arms against his strong chest. He kissed my hair and let his hand run down my back to cradle my ass. He felt the tremor work through me, but he seemed to know I wasn't going with him. When his car came, a dark blue Jag, I couldn't get in. I wanted it all. Every frame. Every image. But he scared me.

Jack didn't mind. He gave me his number. He told me to call. "I know you'll call," he said. And then he kissed me and drove away.

I didn't ask for my car. I was too drunk to even consider driving. I went back into the restaurant and called "home." Garrett answered, a surprise since he was usually out catering—he worked as a chef to pay the bills. "Cancelled," he said. "What's up?"

I'd lived in a desert for years, and now my fantasies were raining down on me. If I'd gotten Nate, I could have explained easily, said what was going on, begged for a ride. Instead, I got Garrett, and I confessed. Crazy desires. I had only meant to explain that I was too drunk to drive, but the words spilled from my mouth, until I was telling him everything. Every single thing Jack had said, and everything I knew in my heart that I wanted.

"Shhh, Samantha," Garrett whispered. "Don't do this. Not on the phone. Let me come get you."

I sat down on the curb and waited, and he pulled up twenty minutes later and helped me in. He looked shell-shocked. "You need help," he said.

"No," I shook my head. "I need someone to spank me. With a belt. With a paddle. I need to be punished."

"Really," he tried again. "That's not healthy. You have to get help—"

I was crying, trying to tell him that I didn't care. I didn't want to be fixed. I wanted what Jack had offered. But not from Jack. Not yet, anyway. Garrett drove us around the city instead of taking me home. He found us a hotel on Sunset. He had never raised a hand to a woman before, never been rough in any way. And at first, he continued to try to convince me that I didn't want what I wanted. But I saw a look in his eyes that let me know not to let up.

There was a huge tub in the room and there were mirrors on the wall, and I made him punish me bent over the lip of the deep tub, made him fuck me simply by explaining that I needed it. I deserved it.

I corrupted him. Evil thing that I am.

But I truly believe that Garrett had the same fantasies I did. He'd just pushed them down. Covered them up. He'd been with the same girl since high school, and all they'd ever experienced together was simple, pretty sex. Now I was giving him the opportunity to open the dark door in his head and let loose his inner demons.

He surprised me. He surpassed what I'd hoped. Not letting up on me when I started to cry. No pity. He was a natural Dom. He spanked me until I felt as if my ass were on fire, and then he showed me my reflection in the wall of mirrors, making me look. I was a mess. My makeup streaked, my carefully done hair all loose. He threw me down on the bed and fucked me, and he made me tell him what Jack had wanted to do. Made me tell him everything, promising that he would take over.

The call came in two days later. I'd landed the job at the salon, front desk, decent pay. The only glitch was the dress code: all black. That was the only thing the owner allowed. So what was the problem? I owned plenty of black—in my closet at Byron's house.

"That's it," Nate insisted when I explained that I couldn't afford to buy a whole new wardrobe. "We're getting your stuff."

Garrett agreed, although he was oddly quiet. He hadn't spoken to me much at all since our night together, and I wondered what he was thinking. I didn't expect him to be my boyfriend now. I didn't know what I expected, but boyfriends weren't high on my list of priorities.

I do know that Byron didn't expect what he found when he came home from work that afternoon: Garrett and Nathan and me, sitting on the front curb, waiting. Byron hadn't taken my calls, had refused to return the messages I'd left at work and on his machine. So now here I was, with two tall young bucks, both wearing solid, serious expressions.

"She needs her clothes," Nate said as Byron came slowly up the drive.

"She should have thought about that before she fucked the boy toy."

"Meaning what exactly?" Garrett asked, standing to his full height, and I saw how much taller he was than Byron, how much fitter. Byron must have realized that as well, because he didn't sneer so much as he said, "Look, I got rid of everything." He shrugged and I felt my heart sink. I hadn't thought of that, hadn't considered that he might not keep my things.

"Let's make sure," Nate said, staring at Byron. I glanced from him to Garrett and understood that although Nate was slightly shorter and leaner, he was definitely the more menacing of the two. "Maybe you missed something."

Byron shook his head. "I've got company tonight," he said. "Why don't you all come back this weekend?"

Nate stood there blocking the door, holding Byron's expression with his own, and Byron gave in. He moved forward, and Nate waited until the last second before stepping aside. Once inside the apartment, it was clear why Byron hadn't wanted us to enter. The place was a wreck. I had been the good little homemaker. Now there were clothes everywhere, and through the hatch I could see dishes piled in the sink. Pizza boxes decorated the dining room table and bags of garbage sagged against the back door. Even more obvious to me was that Byron had been lying. All of my things were still there, although not in the places I remembered. My favorite rose-pink silk nightgown was crumpled on the sofa, next to a pillow and the blanket from our bed. Had he been sleeping with my nightie?

Byron wouldn't look at me.

I headed up the stairs to the bedroom, the boys

following after me. My huge suitcase was under the bed and I pulled it out, opened the closet, and threw in as many clothes as I could. I took pillowcases from the closet and Garrett and Nathan emptied my drawers into them. Knickers and stockings and bras spilled free. We hadn't come armed with boxes. This was true guerilla packing, as fast and as thorough as possible because I didn't ever want to come back. Hefty bags came next, and I tossed in all my keepsakes, anything I felt I couldn't live without.

Garrett and Nathan began toting my belongings to the truck, but I was aware that they made sure I was never alone in the townhouse with Byron. They did this to protect me, but Byron was no visible threat. He seemed to have gone somewhere deep inside himself. As I made my final trip downstairs, I saw him on the sofa, bong in place, staring at the silent TV. But he looked up at me as I headed out the door.

"Fucking two guys at a time now?" he snarled. "You were a whore when I met you. I don't know why I ever thought you'd change."

I wish I could say that I responded with a snappy comeback. But all I could do was feel sick for him, sitting there in the rubble of the apartment, taking solace in a water bong and an insult. The last thing I saw when I left was my engagement ring, shining on the corner of the coffee table.

"What the fuck were you with him for?" Nate demanded as we drove his pickup back to Hollywood.

I shook my head.

"Was he rich? That Saab wasn't cheap." Byron had upgraded to a new convertible.

"Yeah," I admitted. "But that's not why I was with

him."

"Were you a whore when you met?" Nate said this with a smirk. I hadn't known he'd heard Byron's parting words.

I gave him a look, and then the three of us started to laugh. "No," I said, shaking my head. "Not like *Pretty Woman*, if that's what you mean. He didn't rescue me from a rough street life."

"So what was he talking about?" Garrett wanted to know.

I took a deep breath, then shrugged. No reason not to tell them. "This thing happened right before I moved in with him, and I don't think he ever got over it."

"What sort of thing?" Garrett pressed. I was sitting in the middle between the boys, and Garrett's thigh was tight against mine. I wondered if he thought the incident was the same sort that he and I had shared. I wondered if this was the sort of thing he was never going to get over either.

"I had this threesome with a lady from my work and her roommate."

Silence filled the truck. "It was no big deal," I told them. "But to Byron it was—"

"How'd he find out about it?"

"Everyone found out," I said, smiling as I remembered. All the men on staff had treated me differently after that night. But I was smiling because I had never told anyone how much of a liar I'd been. Ava and Charlie had thought that I was an innocent. That I'd never had a guy go down on me, that I was naïve about sucking cock. I had no problem playing pure, letting them feel as if they were corrupting me. I hadn't been with a woman before. That was the only new part of the equation for me. Brock had taught me everything I needed to know about pleasing a man with my mouth.

We arrived home as the sun was starting to set, and we unpacked the truck as quickly as possible, all of us wanting the whole experience to be over and done with. And when it was, Nathan took me by the hand and brought me back to the truck. Garrett followed behind us. The boys clearly had a plan, but I didn't know what it was. We drove down the hill to Nate's favorite bar, a dark dive with a good jukebox.

"Best place to toast a breakup," Nate announced as we snagged a booth in the back.

Garrett nodded and I looked at him, remembering what he'd said about his former girlfriend, knowing that he'd been demolished, trying to guess what he thought about my situation. Rounds of tequila arrived at our table and the three of us toasted.

"To Byron," Garrett said.

"To whores," Nate grinned.

"To my clothes," I sighed. It felt good to have my stuff back. For the first time in weeks, I didn't feel like a homeless waif.

"To threesomes," Nate suggested for the next shot.

"It's called a gang bang if it's two guys," I teased.

"I read that in *Playboy*," Garrett nodded, "but I don't agree."

"I haven't done the two-guy thing," Nate admitted. "Only two girls."

Garrett didn't say anything. I could tell he'd never had either type of ménage. I also knew, from the way I was being handled in the bar, one boy's hand on my left thigh, the other on my right, that it was an experience not far off in his future.

We chose Nate's room.

"What about Lois?"

"She got a commercial. Gone for three days."

Nervousness fluttered through me. I'd been flirting. I knew the consequences. At least I thought I did.

Nate had those ties on his bed. The hook for cuffs. He also had the intelligence not to rush. He told me to take a shower first to relax. My muscles were sore from carrying all those bags, and I rotated under the hot spray, thinking about Byron making love to my nightgown while I would soon be fucking my two new roommates. The nervousness turned quickly to arousal. I dried off and found that Nate had hung Lois's Oriental robe out for me. My skin still damp, I slid into it, then opened the door.

Candles lined the hallway. I walked to Nate's room, so aware of my nakedness under the thin turquoise robe.

Garrett was sitting in the leather chair in the corner, still fully dressed. He had a beer in one hand and a paddle in the other. I shut my eyes for a moment, nerves rushing back. Then I felt Nate behind me, slipping the blindfold into place.

They must have talked, the two boys. Maybe before I was in the shower. Maybe after my night together with Garrett. They must have discussed the things I liked, the things I'd expressed in my drunken confession. Because the evening was completely choreographed. Nate led me forward, not saying a word, and I found myself pushed against Garrett, who quickly took over, upending me over his lap and lifting up the back of the robe. I was nude beneath, and I felt grateful for the blindfold. I didn't have to watch them watching me. I wondered what they thought of the fading bruises on my skin, wondered what they thought of my tattoos.

Garrett set the paddle against my ass, and I could

guess what it would feel like when he landed the first blow. This was a leather paddle, rectangular, much larger than the one Connor had used on me. "Tell Nate what you told me," he said, his voice darker than I'd heard it so far. Menacing. How strange. I'd expected Nate to take control.

"What part?" I whispered.

"All of it."

I realized that I was going to be punished for the first time in front of an audience. Garrett was going to spank the hell out of me, and Nate was going to watch.

"Now," Garrett insisted.

The two shots of tequila gave me a tiny sliver of confidence. But speaking was torture. "I can't—" I murmured. And before the words were fully out of my mouth, Garrett had landed the first volley of blows. The pain was fierce, but I held myself still.

"Don't press me," Garrett warned. "I promise that you'll lose."

Ah, but he was wrong. Losing would make me win.

"It's all I want," I said softly, speaking toward the carpet.

"What is?" Nate asked. He was close, bent on his knees in front of me. He kissed my lips, stroked my hair. "What do you want, Samantha?"

I took stock of my situation: blindfolded, in a room with two men, both who seemed more than willing to make my fantasies come true. What was stopping me from speaking? That same old fear of rejection? Fuck you, Byron. I didn't want to be muzzled by that anymore.

"I want—" I started, then hesitated, and Garrett began smacking my ass again, each slap of the paddle on my skin warning me. "I want this—"

That vagueness won me a series of eye-watering blows.

I wasn't counting how many; I was simply absorbing. Nate held my hands, he licked the tears from my cheeks as they slowly spilled under the blindfold.

"I want to take it," I said, choking over the tears.

"Take?" Nate prompted.

Why did I have to say it? Didn't they see? Couldn't they tell? Wasn't it clear from my body language, from the fact that I had allowed myself willingly to be blindfolded, to be led to a man holding a paddle? I hadn't run away. I hadn't said that they were crazy, that I never would agree to something like that. I had been meek. I had been humble. I had been willing.

Garrett said, "Tie her to the bed, Nathan. Face down."

Oh, fuck.

They stripped the robe off me first. The blindfold was black velvet, and I could see nothing. But it was as if I could feel the candlelight on me, casting twisted golden shadows over my pale skin.

Nate did as Garrett said, lifting me into his arms and carrying me to his mattress. He had me bound in seconds, and I felt relief flood through me. It didn't matter what I said now. I was going to get what I wanted.

"Tell us, Samantha," Garrett said, his voice close to my ear. "What do you want to take?"

I shut my eyes tight. Describing my desires never got any easier. "You have to make it hurt," I managed. "It has to hurt. I want to show you that I can take it. The pain—" I was begging now, but I'd reached a point where I could talk more freely. "Please—" I lifted my voice to both of them. "I don't know why. Just please—"

That was as clear as I could be. The boys didn't need any further instruction.

I'd known Nate had the rigged mattress, but I didn't

know about the closet of toys. Connor needn't have bought the gear at the Pleasure Chest. Nate had the crops, and the canes, and the clamps. But it was Garrett who used them. Was I his surrogate girlfriend this night, the one who'd broken his heart? Was he taking his aggression out on me? Or was I the nymph who'd freed him to do what he'd always wanted?

Didn't really matter, did it? He used a leather flogger from my upper back to the tops of my thighs before striping me with the crop, crisscrossing the marks to leave the most lasting pain. He wielded the instruments like a pro. Not letting up. Not going slow. I twisted under the sensation, but I never said stop. I put my faith in him to read me, to understand. And he did. He made sure I was crying, really crying, before he handed me over to Nate.

Nate had been at my side the whole evening. Had kissed the welts when Garrett gave me a breather. Had let his fingertips wander down between the lips of my pussy, laughing softly when he felt the wetness that awaited him.

I heard Garrett take his seat in the chair once more, settling down to relax as Nate brought his face to my ear and whispered, "All right, baby, now it's my turn."

Chapter Nine:
Fix You

I had felt from the start that Nathan was the one to watch. He had the fierce look, that unflinching stare. And he'd been comfortable manhandling me, climbing under the covers on the sofa, wrapping me in his arms. Not fucking me, just touching me. His face pressed against the nape of my neck, his warm breath tickling my skin.

Now he'd seen Garrett make me cry. And if I thought that there had been some sort of good cop/bad cop routine between them, if I'd believed for an instant that Nate was the gentler one, kissing my tears away, caressing my feverish skin, then I was in for a wicked surprise.

"My turn," he said again, pressing his body into mine from behind. "And you know what that means, don't you, baby?"

I didn't.

"Yes you do, because you and I are exactly alike."

He'd said that before, and I'd refused to even consider the statement. We couldn't be alike. Nate consumed women, took what he wanted from them and left them weeping. He never called for a second date. He was always looking toward the next conquest.

"We're on the very edge," he whispered, and I could feel his cock against me now, so hard even through his jeans. He continued to thrust softly, easily against my throbbing ass. "We like things rough," he continued, "we like to feel everything. We can't feel it unless there's some pain involved."

My eyes were shut even under the blindfold. I was paying careful attention to every word he said.

"I'm going to fuck you," he said, "because you need that." As he spoke, I felt him move off the mattress. I wondered if Garrett was going to watch the whole time. Why wouldn't he? We were a performance in motion. Something that couldn't be stopped.

Nate didn't take off his clothes. He split his jeans and climbed back on the bed, and I felt his cock thrust inside me, lulling me with pleasure. I had endured, hadn't I? I'd accepted everything Garrett had to give. Why shouldn't I bask in the glow, in the sensation of being taken? I imagined Garrett staring at us, drinking his beer, stroking himself, and then Nate lifted a candle from the side of the bed, and let the wax slowly drip...

I could have laughed at myself for believing that I was due to receive some pedestrian pleasure. Believing that Nate was on board for a simple session of in-and-out. What an idiot I was, thinking for even an instant that Nate was the lightweight. No, this dark-eyed player was in it for the long haul. He'd watched Garrett warm me up, and now he, the Master, was taking over. I tensed my back, anticipation beating through me, and Nate slapped my ass, keeping me off balance. What was he going to do next?

The candle wax continued to decorate my back as he fucked me, but I could tell this was simply Nate's way of gearing up. He was only getting started. I shuddered each time the wax hit my skin, and then sighed as Nate rewarded me with a following thrust. He had me teetering on the brink, and he knew it.

Maybe he was right.

Maybe we were the same.

"It's not enough, is it, baby?" Nate crooned, sounding almost sad. "You need more, don't you?"

And suddenly he was off me, and there were sounds of disturbance from the closet. I heard Garrett suck in his breath when Nate returned to the bed. But I had no idea what he was holding.

"Lift your head up," he instructed.

I obeyed immediately.

"Now kiss the tip."

It was a cane.

I'd written about canes, of course. In my nightly pounding of Lois's keyboard, I'd written about all of my kinky desires. Being free from Byron had freed my mind as well. I'd seen these implements in the windows of the sex stores in Hollywood. But I had no idea what sort of pain the thing would impart.

"We'll start with six," Nate said, "and you're going to count each blow."

My ass was still hot from Garrett's punishment, but when Nate ran his hand slowly over both of my cheeks I shivered at the gentleness of his touch. He knew what he was doing. As soon as my body responded to one sensation, he was there to confuse me beyond measure. I didn't think I could tense my muscles any tighter than they were. I held my breath, but Nate was too smart for that. He waited, saw me exhale, and then inhale again before he put his lips to my ear once more and said, "Prepare yourself."

There was nothing I could have done to prepare. The first stroke was fire. Plain and simple. I'd never felt anything like that before. Nate seemed to be smiling as he said, "You've forgotten the rules already, baby? What are we going to do with you?"

Forgotten. Forgotten what?

"You count," he repeated coldly. There was no longer the sound of a smile in his tone. "You count for me. We'll call that one practice." My heart raced. I was in a panic. Six more? Could I take six more? But before I could think to protest, he'd started again.

"One—" I murmured, tears wetting the black velvet of the blindfold. I sensed it when Garrett came forward. He wanted to watch close up.

The cane struck a second time, and I cried out, my back arching, feeling electrified by the pain. "Two—" There was no way I could take six. And there was no way I couldn't. We were alike. He was right. Two halves of the same soul. Nate had seen it from the start. Connor's power paled in comparison. Garrett was a wind-up toy. Nate knew what he was doing, and he gave me two in a row, so quick and fast that I stumbled on the numbers, not knowing where I was anymore, and he laughed again. "Ah, baby, why are you doing this to me?" As if I were causing him serious pain instead of the other way around. "You've got to work, Sam. You've got to keep up."

Ultimately, six equaled more than ten. And ultimately, the numbers were lost in my sobs. You'd think I would have wanted to turn to Garrett for comfort, the way I'd basked in the strokes and kisses from Nathan during

Garrett's whipping. But I didn't want any of that. I only wanted Nate.

My pain. His pleasure.

Nate was on the bed again, and with a tug the blindfold was off and I could see. He undid the ties on my ankles and released the cuffs from the hook in the wall, although they remained on my wrists. He flipped me onto my back.

"Byron should have done this a long time ago, huh?" he taunted me. "If he'd taken care of you the right way, you'd never have been such a little slut, would you?"

I wanted to answer, to defend myself, but how could I? If I said that Nate was right, I knew his immediate response. He would have said not to blame Byron for my own slutty actions. And if I dared to disagree with him, and said that I'd have cheated anyway, he would have punished me for owning my desires. This was a no-win situation. Exactly what Nate wanted.

"He should have seen what was going on," Nathan hissed. "I would have. You and I would have dealt with the situation very, very differently."

I knew he was right in a way. I could see it in my head. Byron had called me a cunt. Nate would have made it impossible for me to sit down for weeks. But there was a false quality to the equation. I'd never have cheated on Nate.

There were clips in his hand now and I sucked in my breath as he placed them, one by one, on my nether lips. The pain was instantaneous—it was all I could think of. He continued to speak to me, but I barely heard a word.

"Roll back over onto your stomach now."

Until he said that.

"And keep your hips up for me." I lifted immediately.

"I'm going to undo your wrists," he said, "and you're going to spread your cheeks wide open for me."

I lowered my head, feeling a fresh wave of fear like ice water down my neck.

"You know where I'm going," he continued. "Don't make things harder on yourself by pretending you don't."

He undid the cuffs, and I obeyed his command, reaching back and spreading my rear cheeks, feeling him watching, looking at me. Feeling more exposed than I ever had in my life. I wished for the blindfold once more, but Nate was too smart for that. He gripped a fistful of my long hair and pulled, making me look back over my shoulder at him.

"Now, beg me."

I could have laughed. I heard it in my head, a bitter sound. Each time I survived one test, there was another waiting for me to pass.

"Do I need to get the cane again, baby?" His voice was resigned. I was doing this to him. I was giving him no choices.

"No, Nate."

"Then do what I say. I won't warn you a second time."

"Please, Nate," I whispered. "Please fuck me."

"Get the cane," he said to Garrett.

Oh, god. No—

"Please," I said louder. "Fuck my ass, Nate."

"This ass?" he slapped me.

"Yes," I stuttered. "Yes, please—"

"Why should I?" He slapped me again.

Oh, fuck, oh fuck, oh fuck.

"Because I need it."

"Why, Sam?"

Images flickered through my head, disappearing

quickly, like smoke.

This wasn't therapy. I couldn't explain. I could never explain. I could only beg. But I'm good at begging. I was in total supplication to him, my fingers slippery on the cheeks of my ass, offering myself to him.

"Please, Nate." I felt as if I'd never stop crying. "Just please—"

I hoped it would be good enough. It had to be good enough.

"We'll get there," he told me, his voice low, and I thought of that night he'd whispered that he'd eaten the girl's soul. Was he after mine? "Don't worry, baby. We'll get there."

And then I felt the wetness of spit on his fingers and the first thrust of his cock in my ass, and I knew Garrett was close by watching, and I knew Nate wasn't finished with me by far. But I shut my eyes once more, and as I found myself coming, I felt him unclipping the clamps one by one and letting them drop to the mattress.

"Good girl," he said softly afterward, touching my damp cheek, rubbing the marks on my wrists. "You're a good girl, Sam." His black eyes flashed. "You made me proud tonight."

Garrett was gone now, back to his own room.

It was just the two of us.

I looked at him, locked on his eyes, understanding full well that we both knew he was lying.

Chapter Ten:
Black and Blue

Black dress, black fishnets, black go-go boots. My hair up in a high ponytail. A velvet choker tight around my neck. I stood in the bathroom and checked out my appearance as if seeing myself for the first time. The salon was in the heart of Beverly Hills. I'd be dealing with beautiful people all day long, and I wanted to do my best to blend.

"You know, it ought to be a collar," Nate said, coming up behind me and putting one strong hand on my throat, covering the choker.

I stared at the two of us in the mirror. Nate had a ruby towel wrapped around his flat waist and nothing else. His dark hair was wet from his shower, and he smelled faintly of a spicy aftershave. As always, he was as handsome as a headshot. But Nate came alive behind the camera.

"Black leather," he said, "with silver hardware."

An interesting fashion statement for the first day on the job, I thought, but kept the observation to myself. I already knew better than to respond with some wisecrack comment. Nate could be unpredictable.

"Buckled tight," he continued, dropping his towel now and stepping behind me.

I tensed immediately, not knowing what he was going to do.

"You're nervous," Nate said, taking my hands and placing them gently on the edge of the pink ceramic sink. "Aren't you?"

"Yeah." That was true enough.

"I'm going to make you forget your nerves," he promised, and I felt him slide the dress up in the back, revealing my bikini panties.

"Aw," he whispered, and I could hear the smile in his voice. "You wore black panties. Black down to the core." His warm fingers slid the knickers past the tops of my thigh-high stockings. "But what's this, baby? You're breaking the dress code."

I didn't know what he meant, and I looked into the mirror once more, meeting his eyes as he gazed back at me. "Your ass is all black and blue."

I lowered my eyes as a shudder worked through me. The welts and marks from his caning and Garrett's cropping were only slowly fading. Nate admired his handiwork for a moment before pulling my hips back against him. I didn't even think to resist—simply gave myself over to him as he started to fuck me, smoothly, evenly, sliding his cock in and out at a hypnotic pace.

"You'll be at the counter, helping people, and thinking about how sweetly I fucked you this morning and how hard I'm going to fuck you tonight."

And now my breath caught, because Nate understood. I could come from being taken this way, but only if he talked dirty to me. "Normal" sex was never enough.

"We're going out," he continued, slipping his hands up under my dress now and tugging my bra down to reveal my breasts. He twisted my nipples as he spoke to me. "You and me. We're going to a special place I know. And they have a dress code, too. Dresses optional. Collars mandatory."

He sped up the rhythm now, pinching my nipples as he fucked me. "So you think about that, Samantha, while all the newness of your job makes you feel dizzy and off balance. You think that tonight, I'm going to clear everything up for you."

And he pulled out unexpectedly, and gave my ass one last slap before walking out of the bathroom.

I stood there for a moment, staring at my reflection, seeing an entirely different girl than I had moments before. Nate confused me. I had thought that after our crazy fucked-up night together, he'd treat me the way he did all of his conquests. That he'd cross me off his list. But he hadn't. Maybe he simply wasn't bored yet.

I looked at my eyes, at the glow in their depths, at my flushed cheeks, and thought, *Jesus, they're going to know I just got fucked*. But one thing was for sure, Nate was right. I didn't feel nearly as nervous now.

Carmen trained me. She'd been at the salon for a decade, and she moved with a fluid grace behind the counter, even on four-inch heels, answering the phones, greeting guests, paging stylists. She wore her ginger hair straight to the middle of her back and had the most piercing blue eyes I'd ever seen—a crystal blue that couldn't possibly be real.

Normally, she told me, she let the other girls do the routine work, but she always explained the system personally to new trainees. That way they wouldn't feel quite so overwhelmed. But even though I was quiet as she spoke, I wasn't put off at all by the chaos. I'd started working in a salon when I was twelve. It was attached to a beauty supply store, and I hung out at the makeup counter so often that the manager put me to work. So the noise, the hectic pace, and the very familiar scents of salons were more comforting to me than almost anything else.

Still, this was the biggest place than I'd ever worked, with celebrities coming in hourly, often using a private elevator in the back. There was an espresso bar and an international newsstand and a whole bank of manicurist/pedicurist stations, chairs facing a wall painted with a detailed mural of a horizon.

"You understand that you never let a client off the phone without booking an appointment. If we can't book the desired stylist at that time, you offer another time. If the time is more important than the stylist, you find another stylist."

I nodded.

"And you're pleasant, even if someone is irate. That's the number-one priority."

"But you can put them on hold," the girl with a shiny black bob next to me grinned. "I'm Nina," she added, "and that's my favorite trick."

Carmen nodded. "As a last resort," she said, "because they'll simply hang up and call back, but if someone's screaming at you, that's what we all do."

Screaming, I thought. People take their hair way too seriously in L.A.

Carmen brought me back to meet the different stylists, and I knew that it would be weeks before I could memorize everyone's names. Half were French, with fairy-tale names like Adrien, Patrice, Jean-Claude. The rest had monikers that sounded as if they'd renamed themselves: Brandy, Temper, Raven, and Frankie. But all were friendly to me as I passed through the massive salon.

"Don't worry," one said, pulling up alongside me. "You'll get it." I must have looked mildly panicked. I stared at him, realizing I'd already forgotten his name. "Matteo," he said, smiling, and when I hurried after Carmen, who'd already headed toward the rear break room, I heard him whisper something under his breath.

"So," Carmen said, kicking her feet up on a zebra-striped leather chair and settling in with a giant cup of coffee. "Does it all make sense?"

I nodded. I'd done reception during my freshman year at an architecture firm. All I did there was run an eighty-line switchboard for six hours at a time. The name of the firm was a tongue twister and keeping the employees straight was a nightmare, but I'd succeeded. This couldn't be half as difficult.

"And you got the dress code down," she said, nodding her approval. "Do you have any questions?"

I shook my head.

"Really," she insisted. "Ask me anything."

I paused. We were alone, for the moment, so I took a risk. "Anyone to watch out for?"

She laughed. "You've got a beehive of pissy hairstylists. Half of them will love you. The rest will try to stab you in the back."

That was reassuring.

"This place has its own atmosphere. It might be sunny and ninety degrees outside, but if KC—" he was the owner— "is in a bad mood, then it's raining in here. There are constant soap operas. We don't have an official rule about employees dating, so you'll witness plenty of romantic dramas. But all in all, I'm sure you're going to love it."

I was sure, too.

The day flew. There was never down time. The phones rang all day long, and the clients came in a steady stream. By six o'clock, I was whipped. At least, that's what I thought, until I headed to my car and remembered Nate and what he'd said. I amended the statement in my head.

I wasn't whipped—yet.

When I got home, Lois was waiting for me with a surprise. She'd landed a part in an off-Broadway play in New York and was flying out in a few days. But more importantly, she thought she'd stay out there. She had friends from college in Brooklyn and Manhattan, and she was tired of working ceaselessly only to land commercials. Yeah, they paid well, but the most recent one was for an embarrassing medication, and she didn't have it in her to continue. Her life's ambition wasn't to pitch STI medicine.

"So," she said. "No more couch life for you."

"Really?"

"Sure, I talked with the boys. They're thrilled to have you as a permanent roommate. You can move into my room, and keep the bed—it was the previous tenant's anyway. And if you pack up my stuff and ship it for me, I'll let you have the rest of the month's rent. You don't have to start paying until the start of April."

I was thrilled. Job? Check. Place to stay? Check. Nate peeked in from the living room and waved at me, and a fresh flutter of nerves ran through my body. Dominant roommate to fuck with my head?

Check.

"You've never been to a club?"

"Yes, I have," I told him. I'd been reviewing clubs for the alternative weekly since my freshman year in college. Coconut Teasers. The Whiskey. The Roxy.

"A club-club," he demanded. "A bondage club."

"No." I tried to imagine going to one with Byron, and the image put a smile on my face. But when I looked at Nate, the grin instantly faded.

"Great," he said, once again placing his hand on the hollow of my throat, applying just enough pressure that the weight made it difficult for me to swallow. He pulled me close to him. "You liked Garrett watching the other night?"

I nodded.

"You're going to be on display again tonight."

And now I sucked in my breath, visualizing the scene as he described it.

"You and me and two hundred of our closest friends."

He faced me straight on then, moving his hand up my throat to tilt my face towards his. "You're going to have to behave right tonight, Samantha," he said, in that soft voice, the one I found most menacing. "I know it's going to be tough for you. But I want you to try really hard for me. Can you do that, Sam?"

I nodded and he immediately slapped my face, catching me off balance, then gripped my arms and stood me steadily before him again. The look in his dark eyes was fierce.

"Can you, Sam?" he asked again, more frightening than ever.

"Yes, Nate," I whispered.

"Better," he nodded. "That's better."

Chapter Eleven:
Reprieve?

Nate had been working on an independent for the first part of the day, and then had gone to his gym in West Hollywood. He told me to get ready for our "date" while he took a shower. But I didn't follow his command. Instead, I sat in the living room with a jelly glass of Jack Daniels, flipping the channels on the TV but not seeing a thing. My cheek stung from where Nate had slapped me, and I had one hand against the side of my face, my fingers tripping up and down over the hot spot.

The JD in my glass got lower as the final rays of sunlight faded from the room, but I didn't get up to turn on the overhead or refill my drink. When Nate entered the room, clad all in black, he practically disappeared into the gloom. I felt him staring at me, but I didn't turn to face him. The glow of the silent TV was the only light.

Without a word, Nate sat at my side. He took the remote from my hand and set it down on the coffee table. I'd landed on some old black-and-white movie, and I stared at the screen rather than looking to my left. I pretended that I was deeply interested in the action onscreen, although none of the drama was registering in my head. None of the movie drama, anyway.

"You're scared."

I nodded. Tears were already streaming my face. I felt as if I hadn't taken a breath since leaving Byron. I'd moved from one situation to the next, always trying to keep my balance. The thought of what Nate wanted me to do tonight had finally slowed me down. And I was terrified.

He took my hand down from my face and traced the tracks from my silent tears.

"We won't go tonight."

I looked at him, at the brightness in his dark eyes shining even in the gray light, at the serious look on his striking face. I wondered why he was taking so much time with me. I'd only known him a short period, but I'd thought I had nailed him. A man who got what he wanted and moved on. Had he simply not finished with me? Or did he see something in me that held his interest longer than usual?

I know my eyes were pleading when I stared at him. I wanted to please him, but my whole body was shaking.

"We'll get there," he said, nodding, more to himself than to me. "Don't worry, Sam. We'll get there."

Now the tears came faster. I was letting him down. Visions of what he'd promised me paraded through my mind: Nate displaying me. Cropping me in front of an audience. Hurting me. And while I wanted every single image that he'd described, I was so worried that I'd let him down, fail him in some way, embarrass him. That fear immobilized me.

"You make me want to move fast," he said, now

bringing me up so that my legs were over his lap, cradled in the safe embrace of his strong arms. "You make me want to do everything at once." Again I felt as if he were speaking more to himself than to me, as if explaining the situation out loud might help him to process exactly what was going on. "But that doesn't mean you're off the hook tonight."

Had I started to relax? Had I let the whiskey work through me, the fire of it calming me?

"Garrett's out until four, at least. Lois's over at her boyfriend's. It's you and me, and I promised you I'd take care of you tonight. I don't ever go back on my promises, Samantha. Do you understand that?"

I hadn't spoken in so long that my voice was hoarse. "Yes, Nate."

"Tonight I'm 'Daddy.' Can you do that?"

Had I thought he was letting me off easy? I closed my eyes as a fresh wave of fear spread through me. "Yes, Daddy."

"All right, girl. Go get your nightgown on and meet me back here."

I dressed quickly. Taking off my work clothes. Slipping into a silky short blue-and-white-checked pajama set. I didn't stop to look at my reflection, didn't pause to guess what Nate had in mind. I hurried back to the living room, and then stood at the side of the sofa, waiting for my next instruction.

"Come here, Samantha," he said, and there was no trace of a smile on his face or in his eyes. He'd turned the television off and lit the tall ivory candles that stood on the mantle. There were enough of the towering tapers to create more light than the TV had, but the room was still dim and cavelike.

"Over my lap."

I didn't look at his face again, simply crawled into position, knowing somehow that no matter what he'd said, he was disappointed I'd let him down tonight. This was why he was punishing me. Or soon would be.

Nate's fingers caught the waistband of my pajama shorts and black cotton panties and pulled both down my thighs. I thought he was going to start spanking me. My body was tensed for the first blow. But he didn't.

"Now, angel, I want you to tell me one of your fantasies. Can you do that?"

"Yes." I hesitated. "Yes, Daddy."

"Your favorite fantasy. One that you've never told anyone before, because you're embarrassed by it."

"Yes, Daddy," I whispered again, squeezing my eyes shut tight as I tried to think what to say. In my silence, Nate ran his hand over my naked rear, and then right when I was about to start speaking, he tripped his fingertips down the crack of my ass, softly touching my asshole.

"Now."

Oh, Jesus. He was going to be doing things to me while I spoke. I got that now. I did my best to tell him. It wasn't difficult for me to think of something to say. Confessing fantasies was what I did every night on Lois's old typewriter. "I'm in a school," I said, "like a private school."

"Mmm-hmmm," Nate murmured, and now he had my cheeks spread apart, and I could feel him simply looking down at me, inspecting me. I wanted to hide, to burrow into the cushions of the sofa, but I held myself as still as possible and continued.

"And I've done something wrong—"

"Of course you have."

"Each time it's different. Smoking behind the building.

75

Making out with another girl. Drinking beer in a car in the parking lot."

"What is it this time?"

"Reading dirty stories in a book that's banned on campus."

Nate had licked his fingertips and was slowly slipping one, then two, inside of me, gently finger-fucking my asshole. The pleasure was immediate, but I could feel my cheeks flaming at the same time. Shame floored me.

"And what happens to you?" Nate coaxed.

I tried to be offhand. I was sure he could see where I was going. "You know, I'm sent to the principal's office—"

"Wearing what?"

"Schoolgirl skirt, white socks, patent leather shoes. White shirt, black cardigan." I could say this fast, because the outfit was the same every time.

"What does the principal look like?"

"You."

Nate removed his hand and spanked me five times in a row. He'd caught the flippancy in my voice. But I explained quickly. "Different each time," I explained quickly. "I'll see someone at a store, or in a movie, or driving next to me, and I'll cast that person the next time I do this—"

"Do what?" He knew. But he wanted to hear me say the words.

"Fantasize. Touch myself."

"Go on," Nate instructed, but before I could, I felt something wet against my asshole, and realized that while I'd been dressing, Nate had gotten out a bag of toys. He slowly lubed me up, his fingertips skating around and around. I tried to continue.

"He says all the usual things, you know. I've been caught. Could be expelled. Whatever. Something clichéd,

I know. But I don't hear a word, because on the desk is this wicked-looking paddle. Wooden, with holes in it. And I know from experience what that's going to feel like, how much it's going to hurt, how loudly I'm going to cry. And I understand that I ought to be paying attention to the lecture, but all I see is that paddle, and all I hear are my own impending sobs."

Slowly, Nate began to slide something inside of me, and I stopped speaking. They were balls, on a string, and I found myself shaking my head. He was touching me so gently, taking care of me, and I wondered how he knew that I'd like this sort of thing. Was I that transparent? Still, as if I had to pay for the pleasure, embarrassment, guilt, and shame built up inside me. I felt so exposed—revealing this fantasy while Nate was playing with me, teasing me.

"Don't stop, Samantha. Keep talking. No matter what I'm doing."

"Yes, Nate," I said, and then quickly, "Yes, Daddy." I tried my best to focus. "He puts me over his lap and lifts up my skirt. He takes my panties down to my ankles, and then he spanks me, as hard as I've ever been spanked, with that cruel paddle. And I'm crying from the very start—"

Nate slipped another ball inside me.

"—and he says he's sorry he has to be so strict with me—with all of us girls—but that we have to understand that he truly does have our best interests at heart. He knows not to stop a punishment session at the first sob. Because girls can fake their tears. He knows how to make a real impression, how to take us beyond our limits. Or where we think our limits are."

"And where are your limits, Samantha?"

He wasn't letting me get away with anything. If I

could focus on the story, I could forget that Nate was sliding these balls inside my asshole, one after the other. But when he spoke, I was right back in the living room, upended over his lap, my pussy a lake of sex juices. My cheeks cherry-hued.

"I don't know," I told him honestly.

"In your story."

"Oh, yes," I said, trying to stay on topic, to please Nate. "It changes. Always changes. Sometimes, I put my hands back to stop him, and he has to bend me over the desk, get something else to use. A cane. A crop. His belt. It depends on what I need."

Nate lifted me off his lap now, surprising me, and pulled my panties and shorts all the way off. Then he bent me over the arm of the black leather sofa and got behind me. I heard the sound of his buckle, and then felt the warmth of his cock against my skin. "What do you need now?"

As he spoke, he started to fuck me, and as he fucked me, he began to pull the balls out of my ass. One at a time, so that I couldn't even think. But I knew better than to stay silent. Already, Nate was training me. My mind worked furiously trying to figure out what he wanted me to say. What the right answer was. I knew that Nate wouldn't be satisfied with a simple fuck session. God, I wouldn't either. But I didn't know what he expected from me.

"What I always need," I murmured, failing, I knew as I spoke.

Nate laughed. His voice was dark. He was slamming inside of me, and the beads were gone, and I felt emptied. I understood he was going to take my ass before he was through, and I also knew that he wasn't even close to the finale.

"Punishment," I said, my chin to my chest, words almost too soft to hear. "Discipline."

Nate agreed. "You do need discipline in your life. But what do you think you need right now?"

I felt as we were playing a part in a script. No, a story. And suddenly I understood. He'd read my pages. The ones I'd been banging away on Lois's typewriter. He was creating his own version of several of my X-rated scenarios put together. And since he already knew what I wanted, he'd know if I lied, if I told him something else. But I couldn't. I just couldn't.

Like magic, he had some thin little switch in his hand, and before I could breathe, before I could beg, he was using it on me, on the underside of my ass, the tops of my thighs. The pain cut me, cut through me. He worked with finesse, slicing that mean implement to the right or the left before landing a perfect blow that made me cry out. And when he thought I was done, he dragged me over his lap a final time, not for any teasing finger play this time, but for a ferocious over-the-knee hand-spanking that left me keening for breath and sobbing without any hesitation, without embarrassment or fear. Sobbing for real. Nate understood. If he kept up long enough, if he pushed hard enough, I'd forget who I was or what I wanted. I'd become his willing partner, his malleable plaything. Or simply His.

I was liquid as he positioned me how he wanted me, dragging me down on the carpet to fuck my ass, reaming me with his cock while I set my head on that soft old shag and wept.

"Does Daddy always know what you need?" Nate hissed in my ear.

"Yes," I choked out. "Yes, Daddy."

"Then you ought to trust me in the future." He was still on me, in me, holding me down with his weight. "I gave you a reprieve tonight, Samantha. A get-out-of-jail free card. I won't take pity on you again." He came in a series of thrusts that shattered me. He pulled out, and I thought he would leave me there, a mess on the floor, to try to gather myself together. But he didn't. He lifted me in his arms and carried me to the bathroom. He stripped the top of my pajamas over my head, so that I was totally naked, and then took off his own clothes and ushered me into the shower with him. I couldn't wash myself, could barely move, but Nate seemed to understand. He did everything for me, lathering me up, rinsing me off, and then when we were done, toweling me dry.

Back in his room, the instructions continued. "You'll go to sleep tonight with my cock in your mouth," he said, his voice so deep. "Like a pacifier. Suck it sweetly, girl, and I'll take care of you in the morning. Suck it like a good girl should."

"Yes, Daddy," I said, as I took up my position. Like a good girl. Even if we both knew I'd never actually be a good girl, I could always pretend.

Chapter Twelve:
The Beginning

Picture me, after years of experiencing no—truly zero—satisfying sex, now suddenly overwhelmed by this brand-new world. New job. New men. New sensation of having my fantasies slowly come true. Or maybe not all that slowly...

Pleasure was difficult to get used to at first. I'd grown accustomed to having Byron angry with me most of the time. Of having to constantly regain those points I was forever losing.

When I was living with Byron, I had learned not to speak my mind. But now I didn't have to hide. At work I made sure to look people in the eye, to be bold, and quickly I found myself gaining new friends. At home, once Lois had moved out, I spent my time redecorating her room—the candy-pink walls made me feel as if I were living in a bottle of Pepto. I painted at night and searched for flea-market finds on the weekends. No angels for me. Gargoyles are much more my speed. And then there was my writing. Lois had taken her typewriter with her. But Nate said not to worry.

"Can't use a typewriter, anyway, Samantha," he told me. "You need a computer."

"Lots of famous people have relied on typewriters," I insisted, as if I were a purist, not wooed by newfangled technology. But the truth was that I couldn't afford a computer. There was no fucking way. I could barely afford anything. The fact that I got my coffee for free at work was a huge savings. I'd arrived in the apartment with no cash. It was going to take me awhile to build up a comfortable cushion.

He left the room for a moment, then came back with a battered laptop. "Mine," he said, handing over the computer. "I had it for school, but I never use the thing. The printer's slow, but it works."

"Are you sure?"

"Look, you need something you can work on. And you need to start sending out your writing."

This wasn't what I'd expected. "What do you mean?"

"I read it," he said, "and I know I shouldn't have." This was rare for Nate, admitting any sort of fault or flaw. "But I was curious, and you hadn't said not to. Hadn't really tried to hide the pages, or anything. They were right there, in a folder on the coffee table. And the truth is," he licked his bottom lip as he looked at me, "it's good. I don't mean that to give you a big head or anything. But it's damn good. And while Garrett and I are out partying or hanging with friends, or whatever, you're in there, writing, every night. I know you are. That's why it's good."

"I can't send it," I said softly. I hadn't been writing for anyone. Except me. I'd been writing because I couldn't not write. The compulsion had started when I was still working for the screenwriter. Whenever I had a free moment, I'd slip paper into the typewriter and start creating a story. Flashing back to Robert, to anyone, to a fantasy that would get me through the day.

"You know what I like," he said, "you've seen my bookshelf and the magazines. And the movies on my shelf. You know that I'm not a novice where porn is involved. Believe me when I say that I know what I'm talking about. Your writing has this sort of breathlessness to it. You can tell there's a soul behind the words."

I felt myself blushing, but I shook my head.

"You need to send it out. And don't give me any bullshit about rejections. I'm in the business of being rejected. Hollywood is built on rejections. Every time I go for a job, I know that 99 percent of the time I'm going to be shot down. You will, too. So you have to suck it up and send out your work."

I was shocked by how he was talking to me. We'd fallen...not into a routine, exactly, but into an "arrangement." He and Garrett and I. Garrett's part of the deal was that he never discussed our two nights together, and if he occasionally sat by my side on the sofa to watch an old movie, if he every so often put his hand on my thigh or his arm around my waist, that was fine. But he still wasn't won over. Wasn't sure. Wasn't comfortable. Nate and I never played when Garrett was around. We were like two kids waiting for the folks to leave so we could have the run of the house. On nights when Garrett was catering, Nate and I would find each other. I knew he saw other women—fucked other women. I didn't care. (Or at least I told myself I didn't.) I wasn't asking for any sort of commitment. I was only asking for release. He hadn't spoken about clubbing again, although I sensed he had plans for me. As it stood, he simply would come into my room or lead me to his and subject me to whatever twisted fancies were awake in his mind.

He liked toys. That was one of my favorite things about him. He liked to surprise me with something I hadn't seen before, something I'd never thought of. A gag. A butt plug. A dildo. (Pedestrian concepts to many adventurous lovers, but brand-new to my bed.) He was open and willing and completely unshockable. I felt I could have asked him for anything and he would simply take care of me. But I rarely ever had to ask. Nate understood. If I behaved flippantly or played the part of a brat, he'd start with a spanking. If I was coy, looking at him from under my long dark lashes, he'd respond in his own flirtatious way, inventing new games, creating new rules. I never knew what to expect. I was constantly off balance, and I relished every teetering, breathtaking moment.

Nate might ask me for coffee, only to take me out behind the café and fuck me up against the rear wall of the building. He might suggest a drive, only to twine his fingers in my hair and pull me down to his lap so that I could give him head while he maneuvered us along the Pacific Coast Highway. If we went to see a movie, it was inevitable we'd have sex in the back row. Even grocery shopping was far from safe. On a late-night run to the twenty-four-hour store, he bought only sex-charged items: whipped cream, chocolate syrup, honey. And while the checker rang us up, he explained loudly to me how he was going to use every item. "You'll be on your stomach, and I'll start drizzling the syrup down your spine, down to your sweet cheeks..." God, he was literally obsessed with my ass, which he stroked possessively in public or private.

Nothing was ever what it appeared to be. If he started an evening off with a sweet, gentle kiss, I knew I was ultimately in for something dark...something dangerous. And if the evening began with pain, I could expect to find myself cradled in an embrace that for Nate was pure tenderness. Even if it still involved my bound or captured body.

And when we were done, if I wasn't too drained (or if he had decided to undo the straps holding me to his bed), I'd head back to my notebook and write it all down. You want to know how I can still remember different nuances, subtle lighting, scents, changes in the weather, the way the cool metal of his cuffs felt on my skin, the way I felt when I heard other girls' voices on the answering machine? That's simple. I recorded it all. Every important moment.

"Send it out," Nate insisted. He was talking about my novel, the first one, the opening chapters. But I was worried. "Send it," Nate demanded. "If you don't, I will."

At his insistence, I polished my first three chapters and sent them a publisher in New York. I chose this famous publishing house because I liked the beautiful packaging of their novels, and I knew that they had writers with darker voices than mine.

"What do you do on your lunch break?" Carmen asked me one day, curiously. "You don't hang out with the rest of the girls, and I haven't seen you in any of the cafés."

The truth was that I took my notebook with me and walked to a bench on Santa Monica and worked. Taking notes. Plotting. Trying to figure out how to write a novel. I'd read enough, after all. I should be able to make this work, right?

But I was embarrassed to say so. Even though people

in the salon knew I wrote, that didn't mean I could claim the title of "writer." I'd told them about doing interviews at the alternative weekly—I'd even interviewed a celebrity hairdresser the year before, and I shared tales about my best interview ever, one of my favorite rock stars. Still, I said, "You know, I'm trying to save a little money. I bring my own lunch and take a walk."

"Matteo said he saw you writing."

I shrugged. "That too."

She gave me a look of interest, and I shrugged and said, "Yeah, so I'm trying. I'll let you know if anything comes of it."

I had no idea that when I got home that day there'd be a message from the publisher. My new publisher. Saying they wanted to buy my book. I was twenty-two. And I only had the opening and the ending.

Nate had already heard the message. He was waiting for me.

"Worry later," he said, already guessing that panic was winning out over excitement. "Worry tomorrow. Tonight," he said, "we're celebrating."

For me, this was chapter one. Chapter one of my new life.

As a writer.

Chapter Thirteen:
Precious

Nate knew the bouncer. We cut the line and headed inside, greeted immediately by a wall of sound and a wave of darkness on darkness. The entire room, from the matte-black floor to the rippling shimmer of the club's ceiling, was an inky black. A powerful band—a blur of motion and electric noise—held court on the generous stage running along one side of the room, its members clad in distressed midnight leather and shredded T-shirts. Black was clearly the new black. The audience moved like one beast, writhing, undulating, but when I squinted to pick out individuals, I saw skin-tight outfits of leather or vinyl. As the lights oscillated over the crowd, the gleam picked up raven hair, gothic makeup, tattoos, piercings.

The outfit Nate had chosen for me was perfect—fishnet stockings, a micro-minidress with obsidian-hued snaps running the length from neck to hem down the front, and high-heeled boots. Nate kept his hand possessively on the back of my neck, slipping me gracefully through the crowd.

If I'd been on my own, I would undoubtedly have hugged the walls. But with Nate, I had no fear of the chaos. As long as his hand cradled the nape of my neck, I felt safe. He didn't hesitate to listen to the music, instead herding me toward a cobalt-lit corridor in the back. I looked over my shoulder once, at the sinuously dancing crowd, before trotting meekly next to Nate down a hallway lined with mirrors and shut doors. I didn't know where we were headed, and I could barely walk in the towering heels he'd chosen for me. But I strove to please him.

"There will be demonstrations later," he said, mouth to my ear to be heard over the white static noise of the band. "Up on stage. But for now, the scene's all back here."

He was right. While my first impression in the main room had been of inky darkness, here I saw a stark vision of skin and metal. Gleaming silver cuffs. Steel bondage cages. More S/M paraphernalia than I'd ever seen—or even imagined. There was lots of action in the room, but zero chaos. Everything controlled. Where the front room had been a swarming sea of people, here there was precise order that felt razor-sharp, as if seen through a plate of polished glass. People nodded to Nate as we moved among them, and it was clear to me that he was a regular here. The unexpected surge of jealousy at the thought of him playing with another girl made it difficult for me to focus on the action around me.

The front room had been overwhelming. The heat from the swirling, crushing dancers. The throbbing, spidery beat from the band. And the intense darkness lit sporadically by spiraling stage lights. In this brighter, more sterile environment, everything slowed down. I was aware of the sound of my heels on the floor, even of the sound of my heart beating in my ears. Nate led me to the rear wall of the large room, where a set of leather cuffs was set up high. He didn't have to tell me what was going to happen. We had reached a level where we were communicating without words. I understood now why he'd put me in this dress. It was off me in one quick tug, leaving me standing in black panties, a demi-cup bra, and my boots and stockings.

Even though there were people in the room—players engaging in scenes, voyeurs drinking in every motion, I felt as if Nate and I were alone. "You trust me," he said, not a question, but I nodded. "And you will obey what I say, every single command, without hesitation."

"Yes, Nate."

"You like eyes on you?"

"Yes, Nate."

"But so far the only time someone has watched you was Garrett."

I worked not to cross my hands over my body to hide myself. I focused on Nate's face, and on his words. I knew he was going to bind me in a moment, understood that he was going to hurt me in front of these people. Knew that by the time we left the club I would be crying. That seemed impossible, so far in the future I couldn't fathom the concept. Yet there he stood, quietly powerful, tormenting me by not rushing through the scene.

"So prepare yourself, Sam. They're all going to watch. They're going to watch you take it."

It was all I wanted. To take the pain for him. And he understood. Jesus, did he ever, as I let him anchor me in place against that wall, kick apart my legs so that I could be more easily spread and bound.

I was trembling all over, my teeth actually chattering, when Nate put a warm firm hand on my panty-clad ass and brought his mouth once again to my ear. "Don't worry, baby. I won't pass you around like some party favor. You're all mine...tonight." Somehow the words eased my shudders, even if I heard the inherent threat to them. "Tonight." Meaning that some other night he would give me over to a different Dom, one of the other players in the room, and that man would take care of me.

I took a breath and held myself entirely still as he tore off my knickers. When I could feel him preparing to start, I shut my eyes immediately, my body tensed, but Nate would have none of that.

"You watch them watching you," he said. "You drink it in."

Nate started with a flogger, warming me up, the tails of the toy landing over and over, swishing through the air to connect solidly with my upper back, my ass, my thighs. I hadn't seen which toys he'd chosen. I didn't know how far he'd go. I simply steeled myself, promising myself that I wouldn't let him down.

But when he brought a crop in front of my eyes, instructing me to kiss the tip, a new wave of fear worked through me.

I looked to my left and saw a tall red-haired woman in a short plaid skirt, thigh-high stockings, and a sheer long-sleeved top staring at me. She held my gaze, and as Nate began to whip me, I found the strength in her green eyes to take it.

When Nate led me out from the back room, the sounds suddenly came back on, as if a stereo had been turned up to top volume. The smells and the heat and the sensation of skin on skin overwhelmed me as we made our way through the crowd. If Nate hadn't been holding me up, I would have fallen. But although my legs were shaky and weak, I felt oddly invigorated. I didn't want to go home. Nate understood without me needing to speak. He drove us up to the Hollywood Hills and parked at a spot where we could look at the lights of the city, then took me out and wrapped me in a blanket from the rear of his truck.

"Your first public whipping," Nate murmured to me, his hands popping the snaps on my dress once more and slipping under the shiny material. His fingertips naturally found the marks he'd left on me, stroking them, pinching the welts before he pulled me onto his lap. I had no panties on, just that short dress, and I could feel how hard he was, even through his slacks.

I knew he was going to fuck me, out there in the cool air, my cheeks still wet from the tears I'd shed, my body still absorbing the pain. But as always, Nate took his time.

"It's like your first anything worthwhile—first kiss, first time drunk, first fuck. You've got to savor it. Celebrate it."

We sat on his truck bed and stared at the city, sharing liquor from Nate's flask and watching the twinkling lights in silence.

Chapter Fourteen:
The Arrangement

When I arrived back at the apartment the following evening, Nate was waiting for me once more. He looked serious, but somehow I could tell that he wasn't taking me out tonight. He sat with his arms against the sunny yellow kitchen table, the folder holding my opening chapters directly in front of him. "So when do they want the book?"

I'd sent in the chapters believing it would be a good six months before I even heard back. It's an understatement to say that I'd been shocked when an editor had responded with a contract after two weeks. I had gone in without an agent, over the transom, with no real credits. No sex credits. Now I had to come through.

"For the fall list," I said, "which means I have about six weeks."

He grinned. "You took a risk."

I nodded.

"So you're going to have to work your ass off."

I nodded again. I was leaning against the counter watching him. I had a difficult time guessing where Nate was headed.

"And I'm going to give you incentive. You do your best work late at night, right? So every morning I want to see ten pages on my night table…and if I like what you've done, then when you get home from the salon, I'll take care of you. You'll have a few hours of play, then you can write for a few hours, get some sleep, and start again."

"What about Garrett?" I asked. We'd never talked about the fact that we didn't fuck together when our third roommate was around.

"Don't worry about Garrett," Nate said. "It's understood."

"What is?" I couldn't help pushing.

"That the two of you were never going to be an item." He stood and walked to my side. The power in his sleek body was palpable. As always, when he got so close to me, I felt my heart start to race. He gripped my chin in his hand and looked directly in my eyes. "I told you right from the start, Samantha. We're alike. You understand that now, don't you? Two halves of the same coin."

"Yes, Nate," I said, my voice soft as I sensed he was already working up to something.

"Yes, what?"

"Yes, Sir," and there it was, the nervous jitters in the base of my stomach, the way my knees wanted to give out.

"You did well last night," he said, "and I was going to take a break on you tonight. But I can't."

He was in motion as he spoke, leading me to his room, shutting the door tight behind us. "I can't, Sam. You make me want to do things to you. There's that look in your eyes. The need there." He sounded half apologetic, half helpless. I watched him from against the door, watched as he started removing items from his closet. I wanted to run, as always, wanted to escape in those first few seconds. But I stayed where I was.

Back in high school, I'd had a crush on a guy my friends and I had nicknamed "Night." He had dark hair and blue eyes, and he held the record for bench-pressing at our school, pushing 350 pounds, more than three of me. At a dance, he came up to me and said there was a look in my eyes that he couldn't deny. Crazy. Every so often, I seem to become transparent, like glass, and someone can see inside of me. We went on a disturbing date together—driving around in his convertible while he told me that his mother thought he might be gay—but the way he had spoken to me at the dance was the way Nate spoke to me. "I saw something in your eyes and I was drawn to you."

I watched Nate as he prepared, realizing that he wasn't going out so often with other women now. Not devouring a soul a night. Had he chosen me? I didn't dare ask. I simply took what he was offering—a deal. Ten pages for the pain I craved and the pleasure that always, always followed afterwards.

Nate knew what I needed. He understood that my fantasies went far deeper than a simple hand-spanking before sweet sex. He accepted my demons and my desires and he worked through the night to make each of my darkest dreams come true.

Afterward, I'd feel limp, demolished. But, oddly, Nate had figured me out. Even after he had whipped me, or cropped me, or fucked me until my body felt liquefied, I could still manage to slip out of the bed, grab one of Nate's T-shirts, and head back to my room. A glass of chilled white wine at my side, or even a shot of tequila, and I was off. Writing. Lost in a new world. Ten pages—2,500 words. The count came easily to me. I have never had a fear of putting words on a page. And I always made sure that I knew what would happen next before stopping, printing off the fresh pages, and sneaking them back to Nate's room.

I got less sleep than I might have needed, but I've always been an insomniac. My mind is clearest around one-thirty in the morning.

Sometimes when I was finished writing, I climbed back into bed next to Nate and he'd stir in his sleep and wake enough to cuff me into place or tie me back down. Sometimes I put my head down on my desk and slept there. Six weeks went by in a hazy blur.

This is what I can say about my first novel. It was short (barely two hundred pages). It was fierce. And I wrote it in six weeks.

Nate gave me everything I needed. Total support in the form of X-rated inspiration and a vicious hand as an editor, cutting parts he didn't like, suggesting scenes he thought would be more appropriate.

The original title of my book was *Dark Secret Love*, from that Blake poem:

Oh, rose thou art sick,
The invisible worm,
That flies in the night,
In the howling storm,
Has found out thy bed of crimson joy
And his dark secret love
Does thy life destroy.

The book was as dark as the poem, as demon-filled.

When I finished, I went out to my favorite bar. It was four o'clock in the afternoon on Monday, my day off. I told the bartender, Jason, that I wanted a shot of tequila. He had names of all his ex-girlfriends tattooed on his biceps.

"Celebrating?"

"Mmm-hmm. I finished my first novel."

"Reading one or writing one?"

I grinned. I loved the question. Who would have a shot after finishing reading a book? "Writing one."

"Then that shot's on me," he said, putting out a glass, a sliver of lime, and a shaker of salt.

I did the shot quickly, no accessories, and then sat there quietly as the bar filled with the pure, shimmering light of the golden hour.

Several tall, well-dressed men in their forties entered the bar. We were the only people there at this slow time before happy hour. I eavesdropped easily on their conversation. They were cajoling one of their friends to have a drink with them. The man insisted he had to go, but finally he said, "I'll have one if she has one with me."

Jason sidled over to them. "She drinks tequila, straight." He sounded impressed, as if I looked more like someone who would celebrate big events with a milkshake.

The guys laughed, as if I'd challenged them, then bought a round. We toasted, their friend shook my hand, and then he left.

One of the men came to my side afterwards. "That was Mr. — who bought you that drink," he said, naming a famous L.A. athlete. "You ought to remember that," he told me. "It's an honor."

After they left, Jason came back to stand in front of me. "It's an honor for them to drink with you," he smiled. "That's what you should have said."

I headed back to Nate that night wondering what our new arrangement would be, now that I had finished. The book was done. I'd sent it off. What was I going to do next?

Chapter Fifteen:
The Offer

I don't know if I've made it clear: I was writing all the time. Every spare moment. When I wasn't working, sleeping, or fucking Nate, I was at that computer. I took Nate's advice and began sending out other stories as well, to *Libido, Playgirl, Penthouse, Yellow Silk, Playboy*. Basically, every publication that seemed an even remotely possible match for my work, I hit with a story.

And then I started—well—hitting with my stories.

One magazine rejected my first piece because there was too much S/M throughout, but the managing editor wrote a personal letter asking me to send in something else. I was elated. I'd read my first copy when I was seventeen, and I was a true fan. Even better, I'd been aiming for the hundred-dollar fantasy section, but when the editor bought the second story I wrote, she used it as the featured story. I made more money from that one piece than I did in a week of working at the salon. But even more exciting to me, the magazine hired an artist to create original work to accompany my words.

Nate was as busy as I was, working on an indie. He didn't seem impressed or even all that surprised by my positive mailbag. Sure, there were more rejections than acceptances, but the stories I sold allowed me to bank a bit of green for the first time. He and I were in an odd place now. I'd turned in my manuscript and was waiting for notes from the editor. I had no need to jam out ten pages a night. Did this mean he had no need to sleep with me? We avoided each other during the daylight hours, still occasionally finding ourselves in bed late in the evening. But I sensed a rift, and I didn't really know why.

That's when Jody called. He was the screenwriter I'd worked for with Byron, and he asked me out for drinks. I was curious about how he'd found my number and what he might have to say, so I agreed to meet him. He was waiting, which was odd—Jody always ran a good twenty minutes late—and there were two drinks on the table. Martinis.

"First off," he said when I sat down in the booth, "I want to apologize. I felt awful about what happened."

I think I nodded. I didn't really know what to say.

"I truly didn't want to let you go, but Byron had been with me so much longer. I actually thought you did the right thing."

"Sleeping with Connor?"

He smiled. "Who wouldn't?" he asked, joking. "No, breaking off the engagement. You would have been miserable with him, always trying to live up to an impossible set of standards." I was surprised that Jody was so easily able to read Byron, to sum him up in a single sentence.

"But that's not why I wanted to see you," he said, "Not really. I would like us to be friends. I always felt you were sort of worth more than him. And I want to apologize for the abrupt way you had to leave. So I'm offering you the chance to use my apartment in New York this spring, as a kind of peace offering. Whenever you'd like. For as long as you'd like."

I hesitated. "What would Byron think about that?" I asked, because there would be no way he wouldn't find out.

"Byron no longer works for me."

I didn't press, even though I was curious. Had he quit, or had Jody fired him, too? Before I could accept his offer of the apartment, though, I had a more important question.

"I'm sorry to be so bold," I said, "but did you get Connor fired?" I had never spoken to Jody like this before. My job had been to make sure his life ran smoothly. If his shoes were uncomfortable, I'd run out and buy new ones. If he felt a hair out of place, I got him an emergency booking with his favorite stylist. I responded to his primal needs. I didn't ask questions or provide him with counsel. And I was never, ever rude.

"Why would I do that?" He looked horrified.

I shrugged. "As some sort of punishment."

Now, Jody laughed. "You ran my datebook for a year. You know what I have going on. Do you really think I would penalize you for doing something so similar to what I do?" He said this as if I might have gotten the idea to cheat on Byron from him, and as if he were oddly flattered. "I had to let you go because there was no way to have both you and Byron in the office, and he had seniority. But I'd never have gotten Connor fired for fucking you. I'm not that vindictive. And you didn't cheat on me, did you?"

"No."

"But I have another question for you. A proposition. I'd love it if you'd consider coming back to work for me after your New York vacation. And not as an assistant this time. I want you to take over Byron's position." He held up a hand heavy with precious jewels. "Don't answer yet. Just think about it. And think about this, too. I have a friend who'd very much like to meet you."

Before I could say a word, he waved over my shoulder. "Here he comes now. I told him a lot about you." I looked around. And there was Jack.

Jack. The one with the out-of-control dog. Jack who wanted to bind me with chains. Jack, who got me drunk but didn't press the issue, handing me his number and telling me he knew I'd call.

"Hey there, Jack," Jody said, "This is Samantha."

People think Los Angeles is so fucking big. Really, it's a tiny neighborhood with overlaps at every corner.

I wondered whether he'd let Jody know that we'd met before, but he simply gave me a wink and sat at my side. "Pleasure," he said, and I felt his leg nudge mine.

"Samantha's going to use my apartment in Manhattan for a week or so. You have a place in New York, don't you, Jack?"

His eyes were still on me, and I felt those familiar tremors start in the base of my stomach.

"Yes," he said, "in Chelsea."

"That's what I thought." Jody was the only one working to keep the conversation going. But suddenly he said, "Excuse me for a moment, will you? I want to talk to the manager about a party I'm throwing for my boyfriend's birthday."

As soon as he was out of earshot, Jack said, "You didn't call."

"No."

"So I had to find you again myself."

"How'd you know—" I started.

"Jody described you perfectly, the dark hair, pale skin, and that smile—and when he said your name was Samantha, I took a leap of faith." His hand was on my thigh now. "I scared you."

I nodded.

"I'm glad," he said. "You ought to be scared of me."

I closed my eyes for a second, then opened them and reached for my drink. "I don't think I'm ready for you yet," I told him, seriously.

"You are," he insisted, his voice low.

"I'm seeing someone," I told him next, even though Nate and I didn't have any sort of agreement about what we were to each other. And now that my book was done, we'd fallen into a weird limbo-land.

"Someone who knows what you need?"

"Y-yes." I hated myself for stammering. Nerves made me seem as if I were lying.

"I don't believe you," he said. "Not someone who can take care of you. Not someone like me." His hand had tightened on my thigh throughout this whole interaction. He slid his body even closer to mine and his fingers pushed into the valley of my lap. We were in the rear corner of the restaurant and I knew that no one could see, but still I sucked in my breath when he started to slowly hike my dress upward, when his probing fingertips ran along the seam of my panties, when he found the wetness there.

"Tell Jody when you're going to New York," he said. "I'll meet you there."

"What if someone comes with me?"

He gave me a wolfish grin. "Nobody's going to go with

you. Because you believe me. You know that I'm telling you the truth, Samantha. You need me. I can take care of you."

Jody returned to our table then, apologizing for his absence and waving off my offer to pay for my drink. "Call me tomorrow," he said, "and tell me when you can use the place. I hate to run, but I've got—"

"A pedicure," I grinned, knowing his schedule at least as well as he did. He gave me two air kisses and hurried out. Jack put out his hand and helped me to my feet. My dress fluttered back into place. "Walk me to my car," he said.

"Isn't it generally the other way around? The gentleman walks the lady."

"But yours is out on the street," he said, "I saw it when I pulled in. And mine is down in the garage."

Jack's Jag was parked in the corner, but he didn't open the door. Instead, he led me behind the expensive vehicle and put my hands up on the cold concrete wall.

"I'm going to give you a taste," he said, his body close to mine, so I could feel his heat. "I should have done this before. So that you'd understand. So that you'd know."

And then he slowly slid my dress up in back, anchoring it in place with one hand. "Pretty panties," he whispered. "Take them off."

We were in public. In the garage of one of the most prestigious buildings in Beverly Hills. I glanced at him over my shoulder, eyes wide, and he gave me a look that I'd seen in Nate's eyes before. Obedience must happen quickly, or there would be pain involved. The thought of Nate made me pause for one second too long, because Jack was taking my panties down for me, roughly pulling the silky fabric along my thighs and down my legs.

"You're always like this?" he asked, and I could hear the tease in his voice. "Always disobedient? Do you always push the rules?"

I felt it was safer to stay quiet. I closed my eyes as I heard him undoing his buckle. What would Jody think if he wandered downstairs to claim his white convertible BMW? Jody wrote about rich wives and their pool-boy lovers. His sex scenes were filled with sparkling descriptions and rippling pecs. But there was never any sort of kink involved.

"You've been whipped before," Jack said, and I felt grateful that Nate and I hadn't connected for about a week. My skin was mostly mark-free.

"Yes, Sir."

"But not by me," Jack said, softly. "Not by me."

Chapter Sixteen:
The Garage

Jack's eyes shone brightly in the garage as he told me that he didn't give a fuck if people saw us. He was going to stripe my ass for me, and then he was going to take me back to his place. I remembered the promises he'd made at the restaurant in Beverly Hills: the toys he owned. The pain and pleasure he wanted to impart. Somehow what I did with Nate always seemed to have a lighthearted quality running through the action. But Jack was like steel.

Jack was different.

I could guess why he was acting like this. I never had called him after our date. I'd struck his ego with a fateful blow, and now he was going to repay the favor with his belt, on my naked skin.

Jack didn't have to tell me to count. I'd learned that much from Nate. He lined the blows with precision, neatly covering my ass and the tops of my thighs. I did my best to remain composed, trying to hide the fact that I was mortified at the thought that someone would see, and wondering how a man who was clearly as successful as Jack was didn't care if someone saw him punishing a young girl in public.

Maybe when you're that rich, you no longer have the ability to be embarrassed.

I kept my hands on the concrete wall. I counted the strokes. It was chilly in the garage and I could hear cars traveling nearby, but I refused to turn my head to look. I thought of the pretty girls from the modeling business on the third floor, thought of the producers and directors at the film studio on the first. Hoped that nobody I knew would see me. I lost count, and Jack instantly gripped my hair in his fist and insisted, "Stay focused, girl. Don't make me angry."

I understood that he wasn't punishing me because he was angry. He was punishing me because he had promised that he would.

Thoughts ran through my head. What would Nate say when he saw my striped skin? What would he do? He went out with other girls, but I didn't think he played like this with most of them. Would he turn against me? Or would he be aroused at the thought that I'd been whipped by someone else? Would he make me recount every erotic detail? The way the leather had felt against my skin? The way my sex juices had started to pool between my nether lips?

Again I choked on a number, losing count, and Jack's low laugh of disbelief made my breath catch in my throat. I wasn't trying to displease him. I was swirling, off balance, unprepared for our encounter. He grabbed my hair tight once more, and brought his lips to my ear. "Oh, baby," he whispered. "You haven't found the right man for the job yet, have you? You don't know how to act. You're untamed, begging for the crop, desperate to be controlled."

Was he right? I had no idea. I felt as if I were on the cusp of coming. If he simply brought one finger between my lips, if he flicked my clit with the softest touch, I would explode. Or implode. I was wrecked, and Jack knew it. But he didn't stop.

The belt kept landing. The pain built. And I counted. Ten. Twenty. Thirty. I have no idea. My back tightened. My muscles coiled. I knew better than to look over my shoulder at him, to try to gauge his limits. I played as meek as I could, arms tight, head down, and I visualized Jack slamming me up against that freezing cold wall and fucking me.

When Jack was finished, when he came up behind me and pressed his strong body to mine, I finally felt the tears come. Not from pain this time, but from release.

He spun me around, and I collapsed into his arms, let him set me in his passenger seat.

Let him drive me home...

To his home.

Chapter Seventeen:
Sunset Over Sunset

Back when I was in college, I got my license to do massage.
I had a table, and mostly worked for Jody and his wealthy
movie-industry friends, driving out to their houses in
Malibu or the Hollywood Hills. My services were often
given as a gift for weddings, birthdays, and anniversaries.
So I was familiar with the building Jack drove us to, an
exclusive condo perched over Sunset Boulevard, looking
haughtily down at Spago and Tower Records and the
glitter of the city. One of my clients had lived here, and I'd
adored doing massages at his place—especially because
Jonah always fell asleep on the table. At the end of the
massage, I'd steal outside onto the balcony and stare at the
lights while I waited for him to wake up.

Jack lived in the penthouse, where the view was even
more spectacular. Daylight doesn't do much for L.A., but
I could tell that when evening came, a magical transfor-
mation would take place. I saw little of the rest of the
décor—aside from noticing that Jack was a minimalist,

which was expected. Hard floors. Straight-edged furniture. Stark modern art.

He let me wander while he fixed us drinks, and again I wasn't surprised when he handed me a glass of very good whiskey. Neat. There was nothing extraneous about Jack. Nothing spare on his six-foot-two frame. No nonsense about his short, dark hair or his ice-blue eyes. He fit into his environment perfectly. But I didn't. I sipped my drink and felt like a wildflower growing in a sidewalk crack. I had that sundress on, a pastel riot of tiny flowers adorning the sheer silky fabric. My shoes were silly, tall wedges with laces that ran up my calves. To be like Jack, I should have had on a sleek pair of black leather pants and a wife-beater. Or an inky black dress with no adornments whatsoever. What did he make of me? Of the flush of color in my cheeks from only the first few sips of the fiery liquor? Of the way I couldn't stand still, but needed to pace to the windows, then back to the nearly wall-size modern painting above the uncomfortable-looking sofa?

"What are you thinking?" Jack asked.

"That I don't fit in," I told him. Whiskey makes me honest.

He smiled, and immediately his features lost their craggy seriousness. His smile changed everything. Lit his eyes. Turned him model handsome. "You fit in perfectly. You transform the place."

I shook my head. I felt like a hick here. The women Jack ought to date ran studios. They had people like me working to organize their pedicures, their facials, their love affairs. Jack had nothing in this place that showed a person lived here. No books scattered about. No trashy magazines. It was like a showroom from an architectural magazine.

He leaned against the bar and stared at me, and I felt myself needing to pace again. I couldn't imagine sitting on the sofa, or on the oddly shaped chair. I couldn't imagine ever sprawling out on the wood to read the naughtiest sections of my favorite gossip rags.

"Do you remember what we talked about at dinner?"

And now I stopped walking. Yeah, I did. Of course I did. He had told me what he wanted to do to me. He had floored me by reciting my fantasies in a way that no man ever had. Not Brock back in school. Not Connor. Not Nate. He had spelled it out, as if someone had given him the key to my diary and he'd read every entry—a diary that didn't exist outside of my head.

I looked into his eyes. "Yes," I said, and then when he waited, "Yes, Sir."

"You weren't too drunk?"

"No."

"What did I tell you?"

I found myself slowly walking away from him, until I'd actually backed myself into a corner of the room— the corner of one wall and the sliding glass doors to the balcony.

"You said that you knew what I wanted. You said I wear my desires on my sleeve."

"But what were your desires?" He was being patient. I could tell. But I could also guess that his patience had a limit.

If I could have burrowed backwards like a rodent, I would have. My back was pressed onto the cool white wall. I was trapped there, but I'd trapped myself. Jack hadn't taken a step toward me.

"You said I needed—" Oh, Jesus. You know? It never gets any fucking easier.

110

"You needed—" he prompted, and then he was in front of me, his hands on either side of me, one on the wall, one on the window. My thoughts slowed down. I realized that he was going to leave a palm print on that pure wall of glass. I wondered if he had a maid who came in daily to Windex. The world slowly stopped moving. His eyes were focused right on mine. I could feel my heart beat. I could hear his breathing. "You needed..." he demanded, and I closed my eyes and lowered my chin, actually folding into myself, making my body as small as it could possibly be.

"You said I needed to be hurt." As I spoke the words, I remembered how I'd felt when he had said them. My legs feeling as if they'd turned to liquid, as if I'd never be able to stand again. My panties were wet. My cheeks were pink from embarrassment. Now things were different. I was alone with Jack. I opened my eyes and looked up at him from under my lashes, as bold as I could possibly be. He was blocking me from any escape. But I didn't want to escape.

"That's right," he said, and once more he smiled, but it was a different smile this time. His eyes seemed to grow colder. The smile didn't light them up the same way.

"You worry about it," he said, looking at me as if appraising my most private thoughts. "You feel bad because of the things that you want."

I nodded, and I could feel tears stinging my eyes, but they didn't fall free.

"Stop beating yourself up about what you like," he said, and his hands came down and gripped my wrists and then lifted them, holding them over my head, stretching me. "It's the way you are, the way you're wired. You need to accept that. If you're going to let me take care of you, give you what you want, you have to get over the rest. Can you do that?"

He tightened his grip and brought his lips to my ear. "You look like you're about to cry," he whispered. "But don't cry yet, Samantha. Let me give you something to cry about first."

Oh, god, oh, god, oh, god.

"But before I do that, you have to trust me." A current of desire worked through me. Jack didn't release his grip. "Can you do that, Samantha? Can you trust me?"

I looked away from his eyes, staring out the window, at Hollywood slowly coming to life now that it was early evening. And then I looked back at the man holding my wrists so tightly, gripping them so that I could not get away.

"Yes," I said, my voice clear and strong. "Yes, Jack."

Chapter Eighteen:
Alone

You want to know what he did to me, don't you? You want to know if he started right there, in the corner of the living room where I could look out, past him, and see the fading rays of gold coloring the hazy sky of the city.

Or maybe he took me into the kitchen, bent me over the countertop, lifted my sweet little dress in the back.

No. Jack wasn't predictable like that. He made me tell him I trusted him. And then he changed all the rules.

"Take off your clothes."

The tone of his voice did not allow any hesitation. With fumbling hands, I slid the dress over my head. I let him see that I had on a matching bra and panty set and the stockings he'd admired in the garage under the bar. And those silly, useless high heels.

"All of your clothes."

I had to bend down to untie the shoes and slip them off. Bra and panties next, then stockings. I was entirely naked, pressed up against that white wall, waiting for

Jack's next move. He only moved very slightly, to slide open the glass door to the balcony.

"Out—"

I looked at him, and I know my eyes were begging.

Tell me. Tell me what you're going to do. So I can prepare myself. So I can process the possibilities ahead of time.

"Out," he repeated, more sternly, and I walked through the opening and out onto the small balcony. He didn't have anything extraneous here. No potted plants. No sports gear. Just a small table and two chairs, where I could imagine that he might drink coffee in the morning, or his whiskey at night.

You think Jack went out there with me. You think he fucked me on the balcony, his test for this evening simply that I would obey him, that I would go outside nude, where people might look up and see me—though from where? Street level was too far down. The nearby buildings were all offices. Would anyone still be working at this hour?

Jack slid the door closed behind me, and when I turned, those wordless thoughts of begging for information now reaching my lips, he was gone. I was out there on his balcony in the dusky lavender light.

And I was all by myself.

I cupped my hands and looked into the condo, thinking that Jack might be on the sofa, watching me, or maybe over at the bar, refilling our drinks. No. There was no Jack. I wondered what he expected me to do. Should I sit down on one of the chairs, put my feet up on the table, act nonchalant, as if I sunbathed nude—in the dark—every night of the week? But Jack would know better. He had my fantasies pegged. He knew that there was very little in my world about which I was nonchalant. Being naked and exposed was not one of those things.

The view from his balcony was mesmerizing. As night began to fall, the lights of Sunset took on their vibrant gleam. L.A.'s constant melody of traffic noise lulled me. I stared down at the cars, wondering where their passengers were headed. To the fancy restaurants or clubs on the strip? Or out to the beach, along the curves of this iconic boulevard?

I wrapped my arms even more tightly around my naked body. How long would he leave me here? I wondered suddenly whether he'd even locked the door. Perhaps he'd simply slid the glass shut behind me, and the test was whether or not I was smart enough to think to slide the door back open.

But somehow I knew. That door was locked. And I also knew that trying to open it and failing would send me over the edge.

I didn't have a watch. The only way I could tell that time was passing was by the sky. Darker now. Darker by the second. Crispness in the air.

"Oh, god, Jack. How long are you going to leave me out here?"

I was speaking out loud, the sound of my voice shocking to my ears. Would he make me sleep out here? Would he leave me all night? What was he waiting for? Did he want me to show him how strong and brave I was? Or did he expect me to break down, to grovel, to get on my knees on the balcony floor and supplicate myself to him? And what would it matter if I did? He wouldn't see me. He wasn't in the room.

Tears started at some point. I was feeling sorry for myself. I'd had an idea of what Jack would do to me, and

I'd hoped that his fantasies would match my own. But now he had thrown me off balance. While I had been planning on steeling myself, taking whatever he had to give, showing him my strength, he had been planning on exposing my weaknesses.

Pacing calmed me. From one end of the patio to the other, my arms crossed over my chest as ever, my hair in my eyes, head down. Back and forth, never stopping to look into the room to see if he had come back. Never sitting on the chair or the table. Not bothering to look back at the view. The darkness of the sky was heavy—a weight over me. I kept walking. My feet were cold. My whole body was cold. My lips were cold. The soft breeze in the air touched the tears streaking my cheeks.

But this wasn't right. He didn't want me to pace like a caged animal. Not really. Did he? He must have been waiting for me to understand. Waiting for me to get the test. To make sense of it. My mind worked rapidly. Furiously. And yet I was at a loss. What did he want?

And then suddenly, a light came on in the living room. He was sitting on the sofa and he'd turned on the light next to him. The golden glow looked warm and inviting. How long had he been sitting there? Could he see me out of the window? Or did the glow in the room create a mirrored effect, and was he only looking at his own reflection?

I hesitated, then walked toward the glass. And then went on my knees, and from my knees to my belly. Head down. Not looking at him. Not even guessing anymore how long he'd leave me out here. But letting him know—I hoped—that I would stay without screaming, without pounding on the door, without making a scene. I would stay as long as he required.

Trust me.

That's all he'd asked for.

Trust me.

And I did.

When the door slid open, I stayed prone, head down, until I felt Jack's hand on the top of my head. He stroked my hair. He pet me softly, gently. "Good girl," he murmured, his voice just reaching my ears. "Good girl."

And then he pulled me to standing and wrapped me in his arms, and I could feel the softness of his shirt, the rough fabric of his slacks, the way his cool silver belt buckle pressed against me. The shudders working through my body came for a different reason now. Relief flooded me, and I would have wet his shirt with my tears if he hadn't spun me around so that I was looking back out onto Sunset once more.

"This isn't punishment," he said, as I heard his buckle undo. "This is a reward, kid. For good behavior." My back tensed, muscles alive and ready. I could understand this sort of action. I could comprehend this type of talk. "I'm going to whip you until you're really crying. Don't try to fake me out with false sobs, because I won't even hear them. I'm going to whip you"—oh god, those words— "until you're crying, and then I'm going to fuck you." His hand wrapped the coils of my hair, pulling tight so that my head went back and my chin was forced up. "This isn't punishment," he repeated, and I could tell that he understood what his words were doing to me. He knew that the words were almost as important as the action. "This is a reward. I'm giving you this because you crave it. You need it. Fucking you without the pain would be punishment for you. It would be like almost letting you come but never bringing you to climax. It would be like leaving you teetering, breathless, begging for more. Am I right?"

"Yes, Jack." His hand was painful in my hair.

"Then say it. I want to hear you say it."

A deep, shaking breath. "This isn't punishment."

"What isn't?"

Eyes shut tight now. "The fact that you're going to use your belt on me..."

"I'm going to whip you."

Oh, Jesus, please.

"You're going to whip me," I repeated obediently. "But that's not punishment. It's a reward."

"Why?"

"Because I need it." I choked on the statement, so difficult to admit, so hard to confess.

Jack brought his mouth to my cheek then, kissed me fiercely, and when he spoke, his words were so soft I could barely hear them. "Don't worry so much, Sam. I need it, too."

Chapter Nineteen:
Need

I think about that word all the time.

Need.

"I need this, too," Jack told me. And everything changed. By taking care of me, he was taking care of himself. I don't think I'd ever tried to envision the situation from a Dom's point of view before. I was so fucking grateful whenever I found a man who could fulfill my own dark cravings that I forgot the other half of the equation: The fact that I was fulfilling his as well. Nate tried to explain that to me—two sides of the same coin. But to Nate, our relationship ultimately had to be a game. He was helping me get over Byron—not the loss of Byron, but the death of the relationship. And then he was helping me write my book.

With Jack, everything was different. Somehow his words gave me power. He let me know that as much as I wanted him to take off his leather belt and make me cry, he desired that as well. My mind tried to put everything in order, but then we were starting, and all of those thoughts disappeared.

Who gives a fuck about need when a man tells you to bend over and grip your ankles? Who gives a fuck about anything, except paying careful attention and doing what he says?

I hadn't stopped shaking since he first locked me out on the balcony. But now those vibrations were electric, my whole body trembling. Jack set one hand on my naked ass, then stroked my cherry tattoo with a light fingertip, and I could imagine that he must be smiling. He was taking his time. He was stretching this out.

Am I the only sub who has second thoughts in those final moments?

Do I really want this?

No, I can live without this sort of power play.

I can get off with my fingers and a fantasy.

I can exist with a book of porn and a vibrator.

But I can't.

Byron showed me what I couldn't take. I was suicidal by the end of our three years together. How crazy that all he had to do was this. Strip me down. Take charge. Make me cry. Make me beg.

But still—in those last tremulous moments before the belt strikes, I have doubts.

Jack drove all those doubts away. "It's going to hurt," he said, "you know that."

"Yes, Sir." Spoken to the floor of the balcony.

"I already striped you pretty good in the garage. And that whipping is going to seem like nothing compared to this. You understand that, don't you, girl?"

"Yes, Sir," my words catching in my throat, my voice hoarse.

"Say it, Sam."

I comprehended this part of the process now. He liked me to speak the things that were hardest for me to accept about myself.

"I understand."

"What do you understand?"

Just whip me, I wanted to beg. Don't put me through this. This is hell. Don't make me parrot those sentences. Don't do it, Jack—

"You're going to make it hurt. Sir."

"Why?"

I actually started to turn around, to let go of my ankles and face him. I don't know what I was thinking. That I might grab him around the knees and beg him? That I could somehow force him to do what I wanted instead of what he wanted? Who knows? I didn't even make it to a standing position. Jack was in motion instantly, gripping my hair once more and forcing my head back down.

"Don't even think about it," he said. "Hold onto those ankles and get back into position."

My tears were hitting the floor steadily now. When did I get so weak? I'd always prided myself on my ability not to cry. Since grade school, when we played rough-and-tumble football. Sometimes boys would cry. But not me.

"Now!"

Jack's icy voice froze me inside. I held my ankles, palms already slippery against my naked skin. And I tried my best to behave.

"Why?" he hissed. "Don't make me ask again. I don't like to repeat myself." It sounded like he was biting off each word and spitting it out at me.

Nate had tried to get me to tell him why. Even Byron, when I'd told him to spank me with his brush, when I'd begged him to put me over his lap, even he had asked later that evening, Why? Why would you want me to do that to you?

Need.

"Because I need it."

"That's right," Jack said immediately, letting me know I'd given him the correct answer. "Take that fact into yourself and hold onto it. Embrace it. You need this." He emphasized each word carefully. "I am giving you what you need. You need me to stripe your ass for you with my belt. You need me to make it hurt. Without that, you don't have anything. You're a ball of longing. A mess of cravings. Without that pain, you're nothing at all."

It was as if he could see those last flickers of doubt in my head and he was intent on quashing each one. He knew. Jack knew. I could make up fairy tales for myself in the seconds before the leather struck, but as soon as he began to punish me, all those fantasies of being normal would disappear. Good-girl sex, the type I always imagine other people to be having in their dark bedrooms every night, with minty breath and cooing dove talk, that sort of sex isn't meant for me.

Yet he waited. Waited until my muscles were screaming, my whole body shaking uncontrollably. How insane that the waiting is always worse than the pain. At least, you think it is. Then finally he began. The flat leather of the belt slapped against my ass, first lightly, then with more power. I held my ankles. I stayed still. He worked rhythmically, left side, right side, occasionally catching me with the thin edge of the belt, leaving welts like those from a crop or a cane. He didn't speak for the first part. He focused on whipping me. My glossy black hair fell forward to the ground. My whole body was intent on not letting go. On not disobeying him. And then I remembered his promise.

I could cry. I could sob. But he wasn't going to stop until he knew I was finished. And fear set in.

How much could I take? I didn't know.

Jack knew. Jack slammed that belt against my skin until I was on fire. Then he doubled the belt and got closer to me, one hand on my lower back, forcing me to arch my ass higher for him. When he prepared to slap the belt between my legs, I lost it. My hands slipped off my ankles, and I placed my palms on the floor instead. Jack didn't say a word—he simply gripped me in his arms, brought me over to the table, and spread me out on the cold glass top.

The belt flew in his hands now. Over and over, a melody of pain blooming each time it landed.

"Now spread your legs."

I did as he said.

"Wider."

Jack leaned over me, and I could feel his cock straining against the fabric of his slacks and the heat from his body, although he wasn't out of breath in the least.

"You know what's coming next, don't you baby?"

"Yes, Sir." Instantaneous response.

"Say it."

I couldn't. It felt like a metal ball was rolling around in the pit of my stomach. Back and forth. Weighing me down. Words are simple. Words are my friends. I can write for hours without a break, without looking up. And yet I couldn't give Jack the answer he wanted.

He moved aside and bent down next to me, face to face with me. He stroked my hair out of my eyes. "Come on, kid. I'm not mad. Not yet. Don't make me angry. I know this is our first time together, first time for real. But you have to obey me. You have to answer me when I ask you a question."

I had my head to the side and I shut my eyes tight. "You're going to use the belt between my legs."

The whistle of Jack's breath between his teeth made me know I'd failed.

I'm lying.

I knew I'd failed when I spoke the words. Knew I was going to fail when I closed my eyes. He wanted me to meet his gaze and say that he was going to whip my pussy. To punish me there, on that most tender skin. To hurt me there. He wanted me to verbalize both my darkest desire and my biggest fear.

He almost laughed. I could hear the disbelief as he said, "Oh, baby. Oh, Sam. I thought you understood me better than that."

And I was in his arms, being carried back into the penthouse, into rooms I hadn't yet seen. Down a long hallway to his bedroom. White walls. White rug. Candles on the armoire. Incandescent light gleaming on the silver cuffs that lay on the bed.

"I was hoping to do this differently," he said as he started to bind me into place. "Punish you out there, and then fuck you. A reward, like I told you. But you have to meet me halfway, don't you think? You have to do your share." He spoke sadly, because I'd let him down. Because I knew precisely what he'd wanted, and I hadn't risen to the challenge.

With Nate, our games had always ended at the first light of dawn. With Connor, the power play had been because of the drama. The hiding. The cheating. The lying. With Jack, things were different. The cuffs were tight on my wrists, the bindings firm on my ankles. With

Jack, there was no going slow. Going back. Going home. This was no game.

"It's my fault," he said, his blue eyes shining. "I thought we were starting from a different place." He licked his lower lip as he looked at me. "I'm not often wrong."

I wanted to beg now, as I saw him regarding me with that inscrutable look. I wanted to apologize, to tell him whatever he needed to hear. But that time had passed.

"You're testing your boundaries," he said, and his eyes unfroze for a second as he regarded me. "That makes sense. Something every good sub knows to do. So we'll start with your first real lesson. Your lesson on how to behave for me." He touched my face lightly, tracing over the ridge of my cheekbones. "I'm only sorry it had to be tonight."

Chapter Twenty:
Secrets

Out on the balcony, while waiting for Jack to rescue me, I'd had a fantasy. I'd seen myself on my knees, undoing Jack's pants, opening the zipper, releasing his cock. I'd imagined blowing him, the cool night air around us, my wet mouth on his naked skin.

Now I was bound to his bed, and pleasure looked a long way off.

Jack regarded me with his stark blue gaze, reminding me for a second of blue-eyed Brock, my drug-dealer boyfriend with the stolen Harleys. Jack appeared to be an upscale version. As cold. As tough. (But if Brock had been in a condo like this, he would have been casing the joint, not living in it.)

"We're going to play a game," Jack said, and a shiver ran through me, although the room was comfortably warm. "I'm going to ask you a question, and you're going to respond." He shot me a warning look, "If you'd behaved correctly outside, I'd be fucking you right now. Remember that."

"Yes, Sir."

"If I accept your response, I'll give you a pass. Otherwise. .." he hesitated, head tilted as he stared at my body. "Otherwise, Samantha, why don't you tell me what's going to happen?"

I understood that this wasn't really a game. And I also understood that we were already playing.

"You're going to punish me."

His smile was as cold as ice chips floating in a chilled martini.

"Bravo, baby. See how easy this is?"

I took a deep breath. This wasn't easy at all. I wished I had my clothes back on. Even that filmy sundress would have offered me some semblance of protection. But really, I wished I had on jeans, a well-worn denim suit of armor.

Jack sat on the corner of the bed. He ran his fingertips along the soles of my feet, and I tensed and tried not to laugh. Laughter seemed inappropriate for the seriousness of the situation.

"I want you to tell me a secret," he said. "Something I couldn't possibly guess about you. Something you've never told anyone." He glanced at the clock on his nightstand, an antique-looking silver clock. "You've got one minute."

I didn't need the ticking of the second hand to count the sixty beats. My heart did it for me. My life didn't flash before my eyes. But my most shameful moments did.

Tick tick tick.

And then, before he could prompt me, I said, "I was born pigeon-toed."

"What does that mean?"

"My feet pointed in. You can see it even in baby pictures. And as I got older, the problem became more pronounced. If I was sitting in a chair with my legs dangling down, my toes naturally pointed toward each other. I walked on time, with no problem, but while most kids' feet go straight, mine angled towards each other."

He didn't seem to know where I was going with this.

"The cure, at the time anyway, was to take little shoes and attach them to a flat metal bar that was about a foot long. The shoes would be fixed at an outward angle, pointing away from each other. At night, I'd wear this bar. If I slept on my back, my feet were pointed outward and upward, to the ceiling. If I slept face down, the shoes would keep my feet a bit off the mattress. Side sleeping was impossible, because my legs would be spread a foot apart and held that way."

"Early bondage?" he asked, and I saw his eyes gleam.

"I don't know why I thought of that," I said, "but I hated the thing. It was awkward and uncomfortable, and if I had to go to the bathroom, I had to call for help. The shoes were always saddle shoes, and I have an aversion to them to this day."

"You walk fine now."

I shrugged. "Yeah. It worked."

He liked this secret. I could tell. It was more shameful for me than I let on. When I was young, I had a difficult time running straight. Couldn't kick right for soccer. Hid during P.E. And once another kid on the schoolyard had said I was retarded because of the way my feet pointed. I worked like hell to get over that.

"Another one."

I licked my lips and thought hard.

"Thirty seconds this time," he said.

"I've never come to pretty things."

"What do you mean?"

I must have turned neon pink. I looked at him, then

looked down, away, around the room—anywhere else. "You're supposed to come to beautiful things. To people kissing. To Jake Ryan giving you a birthday cake on your sweet sixteen. That's never worked for me."

Jack tilted my chin toward him and I saw that he was smiling. "And you feel bad about that."

"Of course." Couldn't he tell?

"You're still there, aren't you?"

I didn't know what he meant.

"The shame is so much a part of you that you can't separate yourself from it. You know what you want, and what you like, and yet you linked yourself for years to someone who despised you for those very desires. The shame of what you wanted made you stay."

There was no response to that. I'd told him about Byron at dinner, although I'd been so drunk, I couldn't remember exactly what I'd said or how much I'd confessed

"All right," Jack said. "Another secret. Ten seconds."

My thoughts whirled. I had no idea what to say. Jack was counting. Backwards. I looked at him, helpless, but he didn't stop. He slowly counted down to one, then reached into the drawer of the bedside table and withdrew a handful of wooden clothespins. I sucked in my breath as he clipped two onto my naked pussy lips, and I could feel how turned on I was when his fingertips gently brushed my clit. I was beyond wet. Jack didn't comment on my arousal, he simply gave me a little half-smile, admiring his handiwork.

"Another secret," he demanded. I'd thought I was off the hook now that he had started playing with pain. But no.

"I cheated on my ex."

"You told me that at dinner."

"I told you I had an affair with Connor. But I cheated on him three times—with three different men. Starting six months before we were even engaged."

"Tell me about each lover."

I could confess this easily. "The first was when Byron was out of town. I went out with a friend I've known since I was sixteen. An actor named Van. I met him in New York while I was on vacation in high school, and we both moved to L.A. the same year. We'd messed around before every so often, but we never were actually unattached at the same time. And we'd never gone all the way. That night we went for it."

"Where?"

Even with the clips in place, I couldn't help but smile because the scene was romantic. "We went to dinner, then started kissing, then drove to some secluded cul-de-sac and fucked outside his car. We were underneath a blossoming cherry tree, and white petals fell down on us the whole time."

"Sweet," he said sarcastically. "Did you come?"

"No."

"Did you ever come with Byron?"

"Once."

"In three years?"

I nodded.

"Did he know that?"

"No. I faked it. Then we stopped having sex at all."

"Second affair?"

"Underwear model who worked at a restaurant I liked. We did it twice, at his house. He challenged me to seduce him, and I did."

"Was he kinky?"

I shook my head.

"Is that what you were looking for?"

"I was looking for something."

"Last one was Connor?"

I nodded.

"How many men have you been with in all?"

"I don't know."

"Better count quickly, kid, you have twenty seconds."
I watched him, now, as he headed toward a shellacked
black cabinet in the corner of the room. When he opened
it, his body blocked the interior, so I couldn't see what he
was getting. My mind reeled.

Brock, in high school

Robert, in college

Denny, the pervert on my floor who seemed to have
memorized my monthly cycles

Jarred and Mark (my first ménage)

Byron

Joe, a boy I'd met while out with Byron before we were
exclusive

Charlie (and Ava)

Van

Cole

Connor

Garrett

Nate

I confessed the list quickly, giving a tiny bit of information
about each man.

"How did you pick up a boy while you were out on a
date?"

"Byron asked me to a Dead show. We went with this
other couple. And the three of them kept going on beer
runs and making fun of the fact that I couldn't drink yet.

Not legally, anyway. They thought it was hysterical for some reason. Byron was twenty-six, his friend Beau was thirtysomething, and Beau's girlfriend was in her late twenties. They kept offering me juice. Even Byron. So at one point, this cute guy in front of me turned around to commiserate with me. He'd been listening. We started talking, and at the end of the evening he slipped me his card.

"Did Byron see?"

"Yeah. He said something about it in the car, something about how poorly I had acted on a date, and I said I didn't think I was on a date, since he was gone nearly the whole time."

Jack shook his head in disbelief. "I would have paddled you right there—"

"At the concert?"

"In the seat. I would have stripped your panties off, bared your ass, and spanked the shit out of you."

I could imagine the scene.

"What did Byron do?"

"Not that," I said, stating the obvious. "He didn't call for a week, and I basically moved in with Joe. But that was a tiny fling, over practically before it started, and Byron and I picked back up."

"Slut," Jack said. "Have you always been a slut?"

I didn't know how to answer that. I'd only been with Brock in high school. Most of my friends were far more experienced. And in college, I watched other girls do different frat guys each weekend, while I avoided the whole scene. I'd never thought of myself as a slut.

Jack seemed to be focused on my list, and I wondered whether he was memorizing my history. Learning everything he could about me. He was showing so much more interest in me than anyone I had known in the past. Asking questions. Challenging my answers.

Suddenly, I felt a clothespin directly on my clit, and my breath started to come faster. I had been lost in my thoughts and I hadn't been paying attention to Jack.

"I asked you a question," he said. "We've already gone over this rule."

What had he asked? Had I always been a slut? It was a trick question. Like "When did you stop beating your wife?"

"I don't—" I stammered, confused as to what he wanted.

"You don't think you're a slut? You're twenty-two and you've been with thirteen men. Most of them within the last four years."

The blush on my cheeks deepened, but I was having a difficult time staying focused. Pulses of pain radiated through my body.

"So—" Jack prompted.

"I don't know," I whispered. "I was looking..."

"For what?"

I could answer this honestly. "For what I had with Brock. For what I had in high school."

"And what was that?"

"A man who knew everything I wanted. Who understood. A man who would..."

"Take care of you?"

I nodded. "Yes. Yes, Sir."

The clips were off with a wave of his fingers, and suddenly he had a flogger in his hand. With a gentle swing, he landed the first blow, softly, between my thighs. Then harder, and harder, gradually building in intensity. In pressure. In pain.

"And the whole time, you've had these warring emotions within you," Jack said, not asking. "You've been looking for what you need, and you've been telling yourself simultaneously that you don't need it at all."

I turned my head to the side, embarrassed at the fact that my hips had risen up to meet the flogger, that my body responded so automatically to the combination of pleasure and pain.

"Is that so?"

"Yes, Sir."

"But what's the truth, Samantha? What's the real truth?"

"Nothing else works," I told him, somehow knowing now what he wanted to hear. "I can't...I don't...It has to be like this..."

Jack nodded. "And I'm going to make you say that over and over until it sinks in. Until you finally get it." The whipping picked up again, those little strands of suede, of leather landing on my pussy lips—and between them—meeting wetness, meeting swollen skin. Jack was punishing me for failing him, but was confusing me with the pleasure it brought. He was giving me a reward after all.

"Tell me what you need, Samantha. Tell me what you know you deserve."

I am such an accepting person when it comes to what other people want. Their fetishes. Their desires. And yet, when I turn inward, when I question myself, the shame covers me like deep water. It holds me down.

Tears streaked my cheeks now. And not from the flogger. I stared at Jack and saw him watching intently, waiting for me to answer.

"Samantha—"

"You have to make it hurt," I said, my voice low.

"I don't feel it otherwise. I can't feel it." Was that clear enough? Would he accept the answer?

No.

"What? What can't you feel?"

"The pleasure. Pain has to come first. I have to take it. Earn it..."

Jack began undoing the bindings on my ankles while leaving the cuffs in place, and I was frightened I'd said the wrong thing, that I'd somehow scared him off. That he was setting me free. I shouldn't have worried.

"Then we are a perfect match," he whispered, kissing my cheek as he repositioned me on the bed.

Chapter Twenty-One:
Consummation

Jack consumed me.

He had known, he said, the first time he saw me. He had known what it would be like to bind me down to his bed. To take control of me. I hadn't been in the same mental place: my head in the clouds, my thoughts a jumble. The headiness of being single and free had been so new, so dizzying. I hadn't been paying proper attention.

Jack was patient. That was his strongest trait. A lawyer at one of L.A.'s top firms, he rarely showed his emotions. Honestly, I couldn't believe I was dating a lawyer. He worked in the same firm as Jody's boyfriend. I thought all lawyers were cast from the same mold. Wore the same types of clothes. Drove the same sort of cars. Got off on the same type of pixie-ish legal secretaries.

Not Jack. He didn't date secretaries. He didn't like pixies. He wanted me.

It can't all be about pain, you know. There is the desire. The power of desire. The want to possess ran through

Jack's veins. He bound me back on the bed, face down, and yes, he used a crop on me. And yes, he made me cry.

But afterwards, he fucked me like nobody ever had. He let me loose except for the steel cuffs on my wrists. He moved me into all sorts of positions: bent over his bed. Up against the wall. Straddling his strong body. He carried me back out onto the balcony, held me in his arms, and drove his cock inside me. My hands were bound, but I slipped my wrists over his head, and he could feel the metal of the chain against the back of his neck as he fucked me. I know it must have hurt, must have dug into his skin, but he didn't say a word. Didn't tell me to stop.

There is decadence in pain. There is a raw sharp edge to pleasure that comes in conjunction with it. For Doms and subs alike.

He bit into my shoulder when he came, leaving marks, making me squirm and grip even tighter to his body with my slender legs around his waist. And then he carried me back to his bedroom, set me back in the center of his bed, and climbed in between my legs.

I didn't know what he was going to do. I couldn't fathom.

His tongue flicked out to touch my clit, and I groaned. He used his fingers to spread my lips, to hold them wide apart.

"Oh, god, Jack."

He tricked his tongue in soothing circles, and then slid the tip inside of me. I arched my body. I begged without words. Jack took his time, knowing how to touch me, how long to make me wait, before letting me come fiercely, sweetly.

He licked his lips slowly, then moved up my body, settling me into his arms, into his safe embrace. He was gentle now, because he could be. He kissed my mouth, let me taste myself. He brought my arms over my head and ran his fingertips all the way down from my wrists to my ribs, smiling at how I shook his whole bed with my tremulous shudders.

Then he turned me back over and inspected me while I buried my face in his pillow.

"You're going to have marks," he said. I didn't respond. It wasn't a question. "And you're seeing someone. I wonder what he will think about all of this."

My body stiffened immediately, going instantly from relaxed postorgasmic bliss to the awareness of a frightened animal face to face with a predator.

"I didn't mean—" I started, remembering drinks, a million years before. Recalling what I'd told him while Jody had left us alone. "It's not official, or anything."

"You said—" and now his fingertips were tripping over the welts he'd left. I could visualize what my ass must look like. The cherry hue. The stripes. "You said you weren't ready for me. You said you were seeing someone."

"I was scared."

I couldn't see his face, and that bothered me the most. What did his eyes look like? Cold and hard, or with that subtle humor to them? He was stroking me in the most easygoing manner, the palm of his hand now running over the curves of my cheeks. Petting me. Lulling me. But I would not be fooled.

"I understand," he said, "but that doesn't change one simple fact."

Could he hear my heartbeat? The throbbing rhythm of it? Could he see my muscles, coiled tight? Could he tell that I was holding my breath?

"Does it, Samantha?"

Slowly, he parted the cheeks of my ass. Slowly, his fingertips started to make lazy circles around my rear hole. I knew what he wanted me to say. I understood my role.

"No, Sir."

"What fact is that?"

"I lied to you... Sir."

"Look at me."

I turned my head to face him, watching as he removed his hand, as he brought his thumb to my mouth, set it on my lower lip. Without needing to be told, I sucked it in, wetting it. He gazed at me, his face so serious, then pulled his hand away. As he continued to talk, he slowly slid his thumb inside me, pushing into my ass.

"I can't allow you to get away with that. You know that, don't you?"

"Yes, Sir."

"You can tell me anything. You can confess any desire. I won't ever reject you for what you want."

I nodded, my body still tense, feeling him fucking me with his thumb.

"But, baby, don't ever lie to me."

Now, I shook my head, trying to show him with my eyes as well as my words that I understood. "No, Sir," I said, my voice a rush, a whisper. "No."

He regarded me carefully before shifting positions so that his hand still had access to my ass, but his cock was now directly in front of me. "Suck it," he said. "Suck it hard. Get it nice and wet for me. You know where it's going to go."

Chapter Twenty-Two:
Over the Knee

I didn't think we would sleep that night. In my poetic world, I imagined we'd be awake to greet the first golden lights of dawn (or, since this was L.A., the first gray light of smog), the way I had watched the sunset over Sunset. So I was surprised to actually wake up, to realize that I had slept, and not only slept, but slept late, long, and hard.

The scent of coffee—my favorite AM aroma—woke me. Jack wandered in, a cup in his hand, and set the mug on the bedside table. I was confused for a moment as to why he didn't simply hand the coffee to me, and then I remembered: my wrists were still cuffed. Gently, Jack unlocked the handcuffs, freeing me, and he rubbed the skin firmly, soothing the marks there, before handing me the coffee.

It was strong and black. I don't know how he knew. I'm a java purist as well as a slut. I will drink almost any sort of coffee. I don't care if it comes from some fancy

French press or out of a bottle of freeze-dried crystals. But I take my coffee hot and black. No flavored creamers. No sugar. I'm pathological about this.

Jack watched me savor the first sip, and he seemed to appreciate my pleasure. He was already dressed in faded Levis and a white button-up shirt, crisp but casual. He looked well rested, but he couldn't have slept any more than I had.

"What time is it?" I asked. The clock was turned away.

"After ten."

I started to move. I'd known it was late, but hadn't thought it was that late.

"Sit back," Jack said, "don't worry."

"I'm going to get fired," I said, my mind scrambling. I'd have to wear yesterday's clothes, which were somewhere in a heap on the living room floor, and I'd have to lie and say I'd gotten caught with a flat or run out of gas, or something. Oh, Jesus—

"I called in sick for you," Jack said, clearly amused by my panic. "I know KC. Don't worry. He's an old friend. We go way back. And I called in sick for myself, too."

I stared at him, surprised that he'd been so on top of things. I shouldn't have been. Jack was always organized, precise. He sat on the edge of the bed, watching me. "You think we met when my dog knocked you down, don't you?"

A spark of fear went through me. He wasn't going to say that we were lost souls from previous lives, was he? That we met because of destiny? I stared warily at him, but nodded.

"Think back," he said, "several years back. To a party at Jody's. When he sold his first movie of the week."

I remembered the party well. Byron had been flirting

with a lady in our office. The one who ultimately outed me and Connor to Byron. I'd watched the two of them together, head to head, gossiping, and I'd gotten drunk. There had been more than a hundred people at the party, toasting Jody. People were so excited for him.

But where had Jack been?

"Watching you," he said. "You had on—"

This I could answer. Byron's older sister often passed her old clothes on to me, and to her, "old" meant worn once or twice. This was a Sonia Rykiel three-piece cream-colored outfit. A short pleated skirt, low-cut halter, and cardigan-style jacket. The halter sagged on me—my chest didn't begin to compete with his sister's fake tits—but the outfit was hot. I loved it.

"And you kept snagging glasses of champagne as they went past."

"I didn't like how Byron was acting."

"Understandably," Jack said. "I asked Jody about you that night. I've been waiting for you, kid. I want you to know that. Last night was no one-night stand."

I was paying attention, watching his blue eyes.

"I want you to move in, Samantha. To get your stuff from that sad little house up in Hollywood and bring it here. I've got two places in L.A. This and one in Malibu. That's where the dog is, in case you're wondering. I spend the weeks here, generally, and weekends at the beach."

I was listening intently, trying to process the situation. Byron and I had known each other for months before I moved in with him. I thought people were supposed to date for a while first. But Jack didn't want me to go back to Nate, to be anywhere near him. I understood this, even if he didn't speak the words aloud.

"You have to accept certain stipulations"—lawyer

talk—"if you're going to accept my offer," he continued. "But I don't think you'll have a problem with them."

Still, I waited, focused, the coffee working through me. "You've dabbled with this sort of lifestyle before. Clearly, you were introduced way back in school. And you've had some fun in the past few months. But with me, things will be different."

He paused, and I took the opportunity to speak. "How?"

He gripped my hand and stood me up. I was naked and humbled. "I'll dress you," he said. "You can make suggestions, of course, and you can tell me your opinions, but I will have the final say."

"Byron was like that, too," I said, speaking without thinking. "He didn't like my pants without pockets. He didn't like my glasses."

"I'm talking about when we're home, and when we go out to certain types of clubs. I'm talking about collars," he said. "And outfits. Special outfits. If I want you naked at home, you will be stripped down. If I want you in a schoolgirl outfit, that's what you'll wear. Do you accept that?"

"Yes, Sir." Accept it? I loved it.

He led me down the hallway. "I'm giving you a little tour," he said, taking me back to the living room. In each room, he revealed secrets to me: paddles kept in the top drawers of chests. A crop in the closet. Some implement of punishment in every single room, always at easy reach. My heart raced as he let me touch each one. I wondered if he could sense how turned on I was, and then I wondered about the women he'd dated before me, the other ladies he'd put over his lap. Had he been with someone at Jody's party? I tried to remember.

"Yes," Jack said when I got up the nerve to ask. "She was beautiful. Think back." And he described her, half-German, half-African, a tall, slender lawyer from his office. They weren't dating. They were friends, both with the same closeted appetite for young, submissive females. "She was the one who spotted you first," he grinned. "But I got lucky."

Jack led me through the whole apartment, and then sat down on the sofa and pulled me onto his lap. I felt awkward being naked while he was dressed. This was something I needed to get used to. My body was sore as well, from being used the night before. Being punished. Being fucked. I tried to remember everything we'd done. Some parts of the evening had become a blur.

"What are you thinking about?" he asked.

I shrugged. "I don't know. It's a lot to process."

"But you accept."

Now I nodded. "Yes, Sir."

He smoothed my hair off my face. He ran his fingertips along the ridge of my collarbone. He held me to him so that I could smell the scent of his skin. I stayed like that, in his arms, as I tried to imagine what life would be like in this condo. I had lived with Byron for three years, first in the Fairfax section of Los Angeles, and then in a townhouse by the beach. This place was in the heart of Sunset, and Jack moved in the same circles as my former boss. I felt overwhelmed at the thought, but safe in Jack's arms.

"We'll go out for breakfast," he said, "and then we'll get your stuff."

I nodded. "But maybe I should call," I said, not even thinking of Jack's reaction. "Garrett and Nate might be worried. I've never been out all night. Not since I moved in with them." There was silence, and when I looked up

I saw that Jack's face had darkened. I felt my heart sink. Was he upset with me? Had I said the wrong thing?

"It's commendable of you to be concerned," he said finally, handing me the phone from the table next to the sofa. "Make the call." There was a pause. "But you'll have to pay."

"Pay?" I stammered over the word.

"Nothing major," he said, "An over-the-knee spanking. No panties. You make the choice. Leave them wondering what happened to you, calling the hospitals, calling your job, or assuring them both that you're fine and climbing over my lap to accept the punishment for caring what another man thinks about you."

Jack was jealous. Nate had gotten to me first. Jack had been watching, waiting, biding his time, and yet I'd left him in Beverly Hills and gotten what I'd needed from Nate and Garrett. At least temporarily.

"Your choice," said Jack, offering the phone again. I sensed which decision he wanted me to make, and I dialed the number with trembling fingers, relieved when the machine picked up. "It's me," I said, "checking in to let you know I'm fine. I'll be home later on today."

Jack didn't say a word when I hung up the phone. He looked at me, and I understood the silent message. He'd already showed me where the paddle lived in this room, in a drawer under the bar. I got up, so aware of my nakedness, and retrieved the weapon, then handed it to Jack, my eyes down, my breathing shallow.

No words. No instructions. This was a test, and I was determined to pass.

I draped myself over his lap, and felt his hand caressing me, the way he had the night before, up and over the curves of my ass. I have—false modesty aside here—a fine ass. In high school, when my friends and I became aware of the more attractive parts of our appearances, it was my signature: Elena has killer breasts. Caitlyn has blue eyes you could swim in. But I have a hind end that men naturally want to cup in their hands, stroke, and in the case of someone like Jack, spank.

He ran his palm over my skin and I could feel the welts from the previous night, little echoes of pain, reminders that I would have for quite some time. Then he hefted the paddle and began to spank me.

Jack was a master, plain and simple. He knew how to create a rhythm in which I was momentarily lulled into believing I could handle the punishment. And then he would land a startling blow, wringing a gasp or cry from me, making me lift up slightly before catching myself and lowering my body back into the proper position.

I didn't count. He didn't ask me to. He simply paddled me until he got what he wanted. At first I held my body as still as possible. Next I squirmed, unable to stop, and he kept me in place easily, gripping my sore wrists in one hand and pinning them in place at the small of my back. Finally, he won the tears of total submission, when I simply pressed my face against the cool leather sofa and cried.

"That's the last time I ever want to hear that you care what another man thinks." Jack pushed me off his lap and over the coffee table, so that he could review his work. "The only man you need to worry about is me."

"Yes, Sir," I sobbed. "Yes, Jack."

"Clean yourself up," he said, giving me one last slap on the ass with his hand. "And we'll go out to eat. I want to watch you try to sit comfortably while you order your breakfast."

I headed down the hall to the bathroom, bare feet on the cold wood floor. I closed the door behind me and started to adjust the temperature of the shower. And when I looked in the mirror at my reflection, I saw excitement in my eyes—pure pleasure that didn't reflect even an ounce of the pain I'd just received.

Chapter Twenty-Three:
A No-Win Situation?

"Tell me about Brock."

I flushed and looked down at my breakfast, a fancy fruit plate filled with papaya, mango, pineapples. Although the exotic assortment was beautifully arranged, my appetite had vanished.

"Look at me when I speak to you, Sam."

I gazed back at him. I had known when he asked me for my list of lovers that he wasn't simply being curious. He had plans. He was a lawyer, after all. He used whatever facts he possessed to his own advantage.

"He's the man who showed you what you were really like, isn't that right?"

"No," I shook my head, scared to disagree with him but needing to explain. "I already knew. He was the first one who saw what I wanted. Who understood."

"And you idolize him for it."

I'm not an idiot. I figured out immediately that this was one of Jack's trick questions. Not really a question, even. Yet he clearly expected a response.

I shifted on the chair and Jack grinned. He was enjoying how difficult sitting still was for me. My ass throbbed from the pre-breakfast spanking. And Jack hadn't let me slip my panties back on. All I was wearing was the slinky sundress from yesterday and those tie-up white shoes.

"I don't know," I said honestly, "we weren't together all that long. It wasn't good all that long. But at the start, it was kind of...magic." It had been. I no longer had to fantasize. I had a real-life, flesh-and-blood man to take care of my needs, my kinkiest desires.

"And what happened? Why did you split up?"

"He disappeared. He'd told me on our first date that he was in 'importing and exporting.' I hadn't know that meant drugs. I was naïve. What did I know? One day he didn't show up for a date. I didn't hear from him for almost a week."

"What did you do?"

What did I do? I cut my hair. And dyed it fuchsia. I wore his sweatshirt every day. I stopped even pretending to care about what people at school thought about me. I got too thin. I tried to track him down, and his roommate told me to forget he had even existed.

"I mourned him."

Jack stared at me for a moment, and I wondered whether he would accept this answer. I didn't sleep. I didn't eat. I refused to speak to people. Did he guess that's what I meant by my three-word response?

"And then what happened?"

"He came back. Called me and asked me to meet him at a coffee shop. When I saw him there, I couldn't even go in. I walked away. He ran after me, chased me down, dragged me to a park bench and started to talk. He said that if he'd told me the truth when we first met, I'd never have gone out with him. Probably true, but I don't know. He had a pack of Marlboros in his chest pocket and he opened it up and showed me the twenty joints all rolled neatly inside. He said he mostly dealt coke to the higher-ups in Silicon Valley. He said he loved me."

"And you believed him?"

I stared directly into Jack's eyes. "Yes," I said evenly. "He did love me."

I knew that if we hadn't been in public, Jack would have slapped me for my tone of voice. I don't know how I knew. I just did. Jack's expression hardened, and I swallowed over the lump in my throat but didn't look away.

"You asked me," I said, "and you told me not to lie to you."

"And then what?" Jack pushed on.

"We went to this twenty-dollar-a-day hotel on the edge of town. Creepy place. And we stripped down and messed around. But it was different."

"That was it?"

"No, of course not. It dragged on for a while. We both pretended that everything was the same as before, yet now he seemed determined to show me that he was broken. Dirty. Damaged. He was more open about his underworld dealings. He called me from jail. He asked me for money. And then he disappeared again, and I went off to school."

Jack nodded, and I felt him memorizing my story. Learning it.

"Tell me three bad things about Brock."

I thought I had. "What do you mean? He was a drug dealer. He lied to me. He disappeared."

"No. Tell me three things that you don't like to think about. Three things that fill you with shame."

He was trying to break down my memory of Brock. I got it. But I didn't like it. I could feel Jack looking at me, waiting, and I tripped through my mental storage and shared what I could.

"When he came back, somehow he'd lost his power. I don't really know why. But he had. He begged me to take him back, and it made me cold inside. I despised feeling like that."

"That's one."

"I flirted with someone else in front of him. I wanted to see him get back in charge, and he wouldn't. He refused. I couldn't get a rise out of him, and I hated him for that."

"Two."

"He tried to be gentle with me. He tried to show me that he could fuck me sweetly, and it killed me inside. I felt wretched afterwards. He couldn't get an erection, and I felt as if it was my fault."

"Not your fault," Jack said. "Stupid man. He thought he was giving you something you wanted, when it was the last thing on earth you craved."

I nodded. Jack was the most focused, the most consistently interested man I'd ever been with. Most guys I'd dated had spent a great deal of our time together talking about themselves. But all Jack seemed to want to do was talk about me.

"Sam," he said suddenly. I'd made the mistake yet again of losing myself in my thoughts, of not paying attention to what was going on around me. "You didn't think I told you to leave your panties at home for no reason, did you?"

"No, Sir." See? I was learning.

"Head to the bathroom, but leave the door unlocked."

I stood immediately and walked through the café to the

single restroom at the end of the hall. I turned on the light and waited. The room was tiled in blue and white, decorated French-style like the rest of the café, with a basket of potpourri and angel-winged mirrors. In seconds, Jack had joined me. He looked at me from the doorway, stared at me in total silence, and then flicked off the light, shut the door, and locked it.

I felt my heart racing. We were in inky blackness. A tiny beam of light from the crack at the bottom of the door was the only illumination. Jack was on me in a heartbeat, turning me around to face the wall, lifting the hem of my dress, pressing his body on mine. I could feel how hard he was. So fucking hard. He bit into the back of my neck and then undid his jeans and thrust inside me.

"I can see you in my mind," he whispered. "This young girl, desperate. I can see you. And I only wish that I was the one who found you first."

He slammed me up against the cold tiled wall. Darkness enveloped us. "I want to know everything about you," Jack continued, his voice low. "I want to know it all."

Again and again he thrust into me, and right before he came, he slipped one hand in front of my body and pinched my clit, sending me spiraling with that glimmer of pain. That spark of pleasure. I pressed my face against the wall as the climax flared through me, and I felt limp as Jack pulled out, tucked himself back into his jeans, and then flipped on the light. He pulled my dress back down, then turned me to face him. I kept my hands to my side and stared at him, waiting.

He slapped my face, as I had known he would. How were we so in tune? I gritted my teeth and stared down at the floor. I deserved it. He'd already instructed me not to let him know whether I cared what some other man thought of me. And I'd told him bold-faced of Brock's love. But I was trapped in a no-win situation. He didn't want me to lie. Yet he didn't want the truth.

I'm lying now. No-win? Of course I won. He slapped me, and I had craved the feeling of his strong hand on my cheek. I had tested him, for once. I had been bold, been cocky, even, and Jack had brought me right down to earth, right down to my place.

"Adjust yourself," Jack commanded. "And meet me at the car."

I nodded and then, on a whim, dropped to my knees. He stared down at me, not looking surprised in the least, as I fumbled with the buttons on his fly, releasing his cock once more, still wet with my juices. The taste of him, salty and reminiscent of my own flavors, overwhelmed me. The warmth of his skin in my mouth made my pussy throb. I licked and sucked from shaft to tip until he grew to full size once more. My head bobbed up and down as I worked him. After a moment, Jack petted my hair, letting me know with that simple touch that he was pleased. I'd taken initiative and he was pleased. Pride rippled through me. My tongue worked around the head of his cock and he sighed and gripped onto my shoulders, but I was surprised when he pulled me away.

"At the car," he murmured, his thumb tracing along my jawline, then resting on my bottom lip. "Meet me out back. At the car."

Chapter Twenty-Four:
Show Me

You can't break up with someone you're not going out with. That's what I told myself, anyway. Jack had a second car in the garage of his building, a silver Range Rover, and I assured him that all of my belongings would barely fill the back seat.

But my misgivings were overflowing.

I felt ill at the thought of the look on Nate's face when I explained what was going on. I'd known the two boys for only a short time. And I was certain Nate would tell me I was acting like a human pinball, ricocheting from one man to another. Or maybe that was my own private fear.

What the hell was I doing? Did moving in with Jack actually make sense? He didn't say a word on the drive, aside from asking me where to turn as we headed up the twisting roads. When we pulled in front of the triplex, I remained in the car.

"What's the problem?"

"Nothing."

He gripped onto my thigh, and I looked into his eyes. "I'm not lying," I assured him, understanding the expression on his face. "I feel odd."

"You don't want to leave here?"

"That's not it."

He waited.

"Nate's going to tell me that I'm making a foolish decision." There. I'd said it out loud.

"Did I have you over my lap this morning?" Jack asked, and his voice was lighthearted, teasing "I could have sworn I paddled your bare ass only hours ago for caring what another man thought."

I nodded. But he'd asked me what I was thinking. And I'd told him honestly. Was he going to punish me for that?

"You don't have to answer to anyone else," Jack said. "You don't have to do what anyone else says You simply say you made a decision. You're moving in with me. There are no explanations that need to follow that statement."

He walked around the car and opened my door, helped me out, led me to the apartment. Garrett was the only one inside, and for some reason, he didn't look at all surprised when I explained what was going on. In fact, he laughed. "This place is crazy," he said. "We've had about sixteen roommates in the last two years."

I was thrilled with the way he responded and headed to my bedroom to start packing, leaving Jack and Garrett in the living room, talking about the weather.

I hadn't actually fully unpacked after collecting my things from Byron. So it didn't take me long to gather my belongings once more, to set them in the hallway. Garrett actually helped us heft the bags and boxes outside. When I returned to the room to do a once-over, he came in.

"You going to leave a note for Nate?"

I shook my head. I was sure Jack wouldn't stand for it.

"You ought to. Seriously. He acts tough, but he... I think he really liked you, and Nate doesn't actually like girls all that much."

He didn't mean Nate was gay. I understood that. Nate took out his aggression on women. He used them. Had I managed to affect him in some way?

I hesitated, and then grabbed my floppy discs from the desk and stuck them into my purse. Jack entered the room and looked around. "Almost ready?"

"Yeah," I nodded. "I'm just checking over the computer. Make sure I didn't leave any stories on the hard drive."

He nodded and grabbed the last box.

Quickly, I opened a fresh file and typed: To Nate.

And then stopped. I'll say it again: How can you break up with someone you weren't going out with?

I looked at the letter.

To Nate. I'm sorry.

I'm just sorry.

Samantha

Pathetic.

Jack was waiting. I closed down the machine, turned off the light, and shut the door.

"You're conflicted," Jack said as we headed back to his place.

"Not about you," I said instantly.

"Good answer."

"I hate disappointing people."

"You didn't leave them in the lurch, if that's what you're worried about."

I stared at him, confused.

"I gave Garrett rent money until they can find someone new."

"Thanks," I said, wondering why I felt as if I'd somehow just been paid for.

"Don't worry so much, Samantha," Jack said, "you can't please everyone. It's not possible."

I nodded.

"From now on, you only have to worry about one thing—pleasing me."

He parked us in the garage, but didn't get out of the car. "I'll have one of the guys bring your stuff up in the morning," he said.

"The guys?"

"Maintenance crew," he explained, "they're always interested in making a couple of bucks. Tonight, let's go somewhere. Let's relax and have fun."

I waited. Jack's idea of fun was something new to me. Besides, I felt tired. I'd changed at the apartment into jeans and a thin T-shirt, finally losing the high heels in favor of one of my classic pairs of shiny penny loafers. But the only thing I really wanted to do was climb into the bathtub and luxuriate in a candle-filled room.

"Come on," Jack insisted, and he led me from the Rover to his Jag, parked at the side.

We didn't drive far. Jack took us down to the curve of Santa Monica Boulevard, to a famous sex toy store. I'd admired the window displays in this fetish boutique for years. Now, we were actually going inside, and I felt both excited and nervous. The place was filled with outfits and toys and implements of pleasure and pain. Jack watched me wander through this fantasy emporium. He didn't give me any instructions. He simply followed me, as if wanting to see where my own desires might lead.

"Anything you want," Jack said, "anything at all."

I walked slowly through the large store, my fingertips stroking different leathers, lustrous fabrics. My eyes were huge.

What did I want?

I ended up in front of the bondage equipment, the paddles, the quirts and crops and canes.

Jack stood right behind me, and I could feel the strength of him, the heat of him. He didn't know why I'd come to this wall. He didn't know about my letter to Nate. About the fact that I already felt guilty for having a secret from him. Day two together, and I'd disobeyed one of the few laws he'd laid out.

"What do you want, baby?" Jack asked, his hands on my shoulders.

I pointed. Jack nodded, no questions asked, grabbed the weapon of my choice, and headed to the front of the store to pay.

"Tell me," Jack said. I'd found myself in what now felt like a familiar position in the center of his bed. Was it "our" bed? No. Not yet.

I was quiet, waiting. Tell him what? I needed more information.

"Tell me what you wrote to Nate."

Oh fucking god. How did he know?

"Come on, kid, I'm not stupid."

I'd broken one of the first real rules he'd given me. Broken it within twenty-four hours, and after he'd disciplined me for this very infraction, as well. After he'd warmed my ass with a serious, over-the-knee paddling. And after he'd given me a verbal warning in the car.

"Nothing," I said softly.

"I told you not to lie to me," Jack said, "and I told you that I wouldn't stand for you caring what other men thought."

"I didn't write anything important. I simply said—" I was babbling.

"Sorry," he spat. Mimicking me cruelly. "You said 'sorry.'"

Was he going to kick me out? Was I destined to be homeless all over again?

I squeezed my eyes closed tightly. I had nothing to say in my defense. Clearly, when Jack had gone back in to give Garrett a check, he'd opened up the computer. He'd seen my damning note.

"Are you sorry?" Jack asked. "Sorry you're not with Nathan?"

"No, Sir."

"Then why did you write that?"

I hesitated, but only for a moment. "Because I felt as if I was letting him down."

"And you gave a shit about what he thought."

I nodded.

"All right," Jack nodded. "Fair enough." And then suddenly my wrists were free and Jack was undoing the bindings on my ankles. I didn't move. I was petrified.

"Go," he said. "Go."

"Jack, please..."

"If you want to be with him, I won't stop you."

"Please, Jack..."

He stood there, looking at me. I sat up on the bed, wrapped my arms around my naked body, curled as tightly into a ball as I could possibly get, as cold as I'd been naked in the night air on Jack's balcony.

"I'm sure he'll take you back."

"I don't want to go."

Jack stared at me in silence, and I wondered which one of us would speak first. But I shouldn't have. Of course, it would be me. "Please, Jack." I got off the bed and bent down in front of him. "Please, Jack. I'm sorry."

"That's what you said to Nate."

Ah, fuck me.

"I had to say something."

"No, you didn't. You could have left. He'd have understood that message perfectly."

I didn't know what to do. I couldn't get any lower on the floor than I was. I couldn't get any more stripped down. I was entirely naked and crying, and all I could imagine was Jack pushing me outside into the hallway and leaving me there.

"You want to stay with me?" he finally asked.

"Yes, yes," babbling again. "Yes, Sir. Please, Sir."

"Then show me."

I didn't immediately know what he meant, what he wanted. I was already groveling. Nude. Begging. But then inspiration hit, and I climbed back on the bed and put my hands over my head, wrists together. Everything seemed clear to me. Show him. I'd asked him to buy the cane. I'd picked the thing out myself. And now I would take the punishment. Without needing to be tied. Without having to be bound.

Jack made me wait. Yes, he made me wait.

But for the first time, I was ready.

Chapter Twenty-Five:
Three-AM Wake-Up Call

It took several days before I remembered I'd left my car outside the bar. Yes, I'm ditzy, but this was different. There hadn't been a need for me to drive, and there hadn't been a moment for me to worry. Jack had arranged the week so that we both had time off, and he chauffeured us wherever we needed to go. But this was one of those three-AM revelations, when I sat up in bed, waking Jack, then flipped on the light on the nightstand.

"What's wrong?"

"My car," I told him. "It's probably been impounded and towed away by now."

Jack started to laugh, pulling me back down under the covers with him. "Don't worry, Sam. I took care of it."

"How?"

He looked at me in that casual way, appraising. "You don't have faith in me yet, do you?"

I always seemed to walk into things with Jack. I thought we'd been talking about my car. Suddenly, we were talking about the two of us. I knew by now to weigh my words carefully, to consider my response.

"Yes, I have faith," I told him.

"Then why do you think I'd let your car get impounded?"

I waited to see where he was going with this.

"It's at my place in Malibu. I had my assistant drive it there the first night you stayed over."

"How?" I started. "How did you know?"

Jack shrugged. "I told you, Samantha. At the restaurant, I told you what you wanted. I told you I could give you everything you needed. I wasn't going to take a second chance and let you get away." He pulled me into his arms while I thought about what he'd said. Somehow he'd gotten the keys to my car—from my purse? Or had he called AAA? He'd gotten my car, one way or another. Before he'd even asked me to move in with him, he'd already known what my answer would be. Was that always the case? Were the questions he asked me out of politeness alone? Did I ever actually have a choice?

I could still feel Jack looking at me, and I wondered whether he could guess what I was thinking. He was good at this game. Sometimes he understood my concerns, my worries, before I even did myself.

"I would have had your car delivered to you," he said. "I would have let you go, no questions asked, no hard feelings."

"But now..." I said. We'd had a frivolous couple of days, with Jack taking me shopping, buying me high-heeled shoes and armfuls of lingerie, collars, leashes, toys. He had gone easy on me since we'd returned from the boys' apartment, and although I still wore the bruises from the cane like badges of honor, he hadn't done more than spank me.

"Do you want to leave?"

"No, Sir."

"Then what's the problem, Sam?"

I didn't have a problem. And I couldn't verbalize my question. How unprofessional for a writer to be unable to find the words.

"You want to know where you stand," he said, and he moved so that he was sitting up in the bed, bolstered by the pillows, and he pulled me over his lap. I could feel myself getting instantly wet. I can't tell you why being spanked is such a fucking turn-on for me. But I can tell you that Jack was the best—at the build-up, the anticipation. At drawing out every second of a scene. He put me over his lap now for no reason at all except that he liked to spank me. I knew he wasn't punishing me for waking him up, although he could have used that as an excuse if he'd wanted. "Three in the morning is not the appropriate time for a serious discussion." He could have said anything. Instead, he simply lifted the new, sheer little nightie and started to stroke my naked ass, his warm hand lingering on the curves of my cheeks. I didn't have on any panties. Jack liked me to sleep semi-nude.

"You were in the equivalent of a Master/sub relationship with Byron," he said, as if telling me a bedtime story. He slapped my ass once, as if the name Byron incensed him, and I squirmed but caught myself quickly, on guard. "Except that he never gave you what you wanted. He controlled you. He domesticated you. But his punishment was by far crueler than mine will ever be."

It was awe-inspiring how well he understood. Summing up Byron so easily.

"I don't want you to be silent," Jack said. "If you have something to say to me, say it. If you have an issue, spell it out. If you don't like what I'm doing or where I'm going, you're free to speak. You should never be afraid of me in that manner." He spanked me again and then paused, and I could guess he was admiring the blush coloring my rear cheeks.

"Don't lie to me. Don't cheat on me. Don't flirt with another man. And we'll be fine."

I took a breath, wondering if it was okay to talk now. I was ass-up over his lap, in a very indelicate position. I pushed past my fear and said, "You do everything for me. It's a little difficult to get used to."

He laughed. "So I like to pamper you. Sue me. I'll let you take care of me in other ways."

I'll say here that I wasn't some girl plucked from the cinders, unused to the whirlwind lifestyle of the rich and famous. Byron came from extreme wealth. His father's place was in Bel Air. When Byron and I traveled, we went first class—to luxurious beaches and faraway ski resorts. But I'm a working-class girl at heart. I've always been more comfortable hanging out with guys who work at grocery stores and coffee shops and garages. Still, with Jack, the money didn't seem to mean much to him. He didn't flaunt it or brag about it. He used the cash as a vehicle to get what he wanted: treats for the two of us.

He spanked me rapidly then, bringing me back to the present with that vibrant spark of pain. And finally I was able to voice the one thing that had worried me.

"What about my writing?" This was a whisper. Jack stopped spanking me, and his hand returned to making those gentle strokes up and over my now-smarting rear.

"That's yours. All yours. You tell me you have to work

and I'll back off. You tell me you need my help, and I'll give you a hundred percent. I won't interfere in any way."

And that was somehow all I needed to hear. And once again, we were off...

Jack spanked me until my ass throbbed, over and over, winning sobs from my lips at the power behind each blow—and then he reached into the nightstand drawer. "Close your eyes," he demanded, and I did what he said. I felt the cool shock of lube and then Jack's fingers pushing one anal bead after another into my ass. Embarrassment turned my face as dark cherry as my ass. But Jack didn't hesitate or go slow. He slid the entire string of beads into my hole, and then he resumed the spanking, this time with one of his favorite weapons: a wooden ruler.

I knew by now what the toys meant. He was going to fuck my ass when he was finished. That thought made me wetter even than the spanking did.

"Off," Jack said suddenly, pushing me from his lap. "I want you on your hands and knees in the center of the bed."

I obeyed immediately.

"Now, I'm going to watch as you pull out those beads."

Life was always a surprise with Jack. It would have been so much easier for me if he did everything. Treating me like a toy, a plaything, not making me take an active part.

"Now—"

Slowly, I reached around to grab the end of the beads. I looked away from Jack as I pulled the first one out, but he gripped me by the hair and turned my face toward his.

"I want to watch," he said. "I want to see your dark eyes glow as you pull those free, and I want to see you thinking about how my cock is going to feel inside your asshole."

I stared into his blue eyes as I pulled out the next bead, and the next, and then Jack was in motion, for once unable to wait. He took his position behind me on the bed, and he pulled the rest out in rapid succession, leaving me breathless, and then drove his cock inside of me.

Ah, fuck. The feeling of him slamming into my well-tanned ass was surreal. And what he said next brought me right to the edge.

"We're going shopping again soon," Jack said as he fucked me. "For butt plugs. I want to get a range of sizes, and I want to try them out on you. One after the other. I want to find the ones for pleasure and the ones for punishment, and then we'll choose your favorite and I'll make you wear it out."

He strummed my clit as he spoke, and I came, squeezing him so tightly that I brought him to climax with me. And then there were no words. Just the thrusting of Jack inside of me, the power of his release as he collapsed on my body and pinned me down to the bed.

Neither of us had the strength to turn the light back off. It was still on when we woke up in the morning, sunlight stealing across the blankets in rippling rows of gold.

Chapter Twenty-Six:
Spank Me, Jack

Jack stayed true to his word. He dictated what we did for fun, how I dressed when we went out, and how we played. But whenever I sat down at his computer to work, he left me alone. He didn't pace or interrupt. He didn't try to woo me away with decadent diversions. Often he went back to his office to work, as well. Or out to the gym. Or for a run on the beach, if we were in Malibu.

He didn't ask to read what I was working on, either, although he was more than happy to offer critiques if I requested his opinion. And when it came time for me to go to New York to meet with my publisher, he didn't take over.

"Do you want to stay at my place?"

"Not without you," I told him.

'So you'll use Jody's?"

I shook my head. I felt strange accepting his offer. It would put me in my former boss's debt, and for the first time, I felt on equal footing with him. I hadn't yet decided whether to go back to work in his office.

"A hotel," I said. My whole book deal would barely cover the trip to New York, but I wanted to travel in class. Jack nodded.

"I wish I could go with you," he said, "but work—" and he trailed off. I understood after that first week what an effort it had been for him to take a vacation. He was driven, and relaxation didn't come easily for him. I also understood it showed supreme restraint on his part to be so laid back about me traveling without him. He watched me pack, looking over my suitcase in silence.

"What?" I finally asked. "What's wrong?"

"You're only bringing black."

"Yeah, I know."

"It's sort of morbid."

"It's New York."

I'd been to Manhattan often enough to appreciate the different dress styles of the coasts. Where you can wear flirty sundresses all year round in L.A., New York's a much more dramatic environment.

"I like you in color."

"You're not even going to be there," I grinned at him. "How will it bother you if I'm all in black?"

"I'll know," he said, teasing me. "I'll feel it."

Jack had gotten me time off at the salon. He actually didn't want me to go back to KC's, didn't want me to work at all. He felt that if I was going to be a writer, I should focus on writing. But I've never worked that way. I like diversions. I couldn't sit at a computer for ten hours straight. My mind is often focused on projects even when I'm away from my desk. Still, he'd arranged for me to have time off, to think about my options: the salon, Jody, or letting Jack take care of everything.

* * *

The hotel is gone now, to my supreme distress. But it was my favorite spot in New York. So hip, with the most beautiful staff and an ultra-chic lounge. The elevators were lit in red, orange, purple, and green. The bar was insane. So dark. So sexy. And the tiny little guest rooms charmed me with their black-and-white checked floors, boasting only enough space for a bed and a miniscule dresser. A huge painting took up the wall behind the bed, adding the only color to the room.

I fit in perfectly in my black attire, as I'd known I would. I felt a rush of freedom as I walked through the city. I had three appointments over the next few days with my new publisher and two magazines. But I had nowhere to be that first afternoon, and I walked through the neighborhood, trying to decide what to do. Where to go.

It's not surprising that I ended up in the hotel bar at the counter, trying to read in the dim light and failing. I had my manuscript with me, the revised one that I was going to turn in to my publisher in person. I drank tequila slowly, savoring the sensation. Several boys flirted with me, but I brushed them off. I wasn't interested in a New York fling. Not with Jack waiting at home.

Thank fucking god.

When I went back up to the room, I was sweetly tipsy, but not drunk. I got my key in the lock and opened the door to find Jack—on the bed, fully dressed, reading the paper. He smiled at me as I stood there in shock.

"I couldn't," he said. "After you left this morning, I booked the next flight." He stood up and pulled me into his arms. "I couldn't—"

The room was so small, and with Jack, his height, his power, it seemed smaller still. I thought about the boys in

169

the bar and wondered if Jack had come because he didn't trust me. But I didn't ask. The answer wouldn't have done me any good.

"Where were you?" he murmured as he kissed my neck. "I've been up here an hour."

"I was downstairs." I pulled away from him, so that I could set down my purse and the folder holding my manuscript and take off my sweater. "In the bar."

He kissed my lips, tasting the tequila.

"You've been a good girl?"

And there it was.

"Of course."

"Not chatting up any local bucks." This wasn't a question.

He'd seen me. That was obvious. He might even have been in the bar with me. The room was so dark and I'd gotten myself a corner spot. I hadn't been looking around at all, because I hadn't been expecting Jack.

"A few guys tried to buy me drinks, but I didn't let them."

"No," Jack said, pulling now on my dress, tugging at the tie on the side and then flipping open the two buttons so that the fabric came off in a wave. "You wouldn't have let another man buy you a drink." I was in my stockings— black, sheer—and these beautiful, high-heeled Mary Janes. My bra and panties were matching black satin, and I had on a thin beaded choker, my only jewelry. Jack slid one finger under the necklace, testing it, and then spun me around and undid the clasp. He must have been carrying the collar in his pocket, because I felt him buckle the thick leather into place. Had he carried the collar on the plane, stroking the buckle absentmindedly as he drank his first-class champagne?

170

"Now," Jack said, spinning me around and then standing back, admiring me. "What should I do to you first?"

I felt my cheeks flush, and I looked down at the ground. Truth? I was thrilled he had surprised me. Although being in New York on my own had felt empowering, it had also been supremely lonely.

"I asked you a question." Jack's voice was soft, almost taunting. I raised my eyes to look at him. "What should I do to you...first?"

My heart raced. Did he really want me to say? I hesitated for one more moment, but when it became obvious that Jack was actually waiting for my response, I reached out and let my fingers trace the ridge of his belt buckle.

"Undo the buckle," Jack commanded.

I took a step closer and worked the buckle for him.

"Now take off the belt."

I pulled, freeing the leather from the loops of his slacks.

"Double it up..."

Jack was clearly enjoying himself. I folded the leather in half

"...and give yourself a good, firm smack on the thigh."

I looked at him, pleading, but Jack's eyes had gone that cold route, and there was no sense in trying to dissuade him. I pulled back my hand and slapped the leather hard against my upper thigh. I knew to strike as fiercely as I could. Going soft or easy would be an insult to Jack. He came closer and inspected the immediate stripe blooming on my pale skin.

"Again."

I obeyed immediately.

"Now tell me," Jack said. "What should I do to you first?"

I handed him the belt, pushed it into his hands. I didn't say please. I didn't say *You know, Jack. Don't make me...* I said, simply and clearly, "Spank me, Jack."

"But why should I? You didn't flirt with the boys. You didn't do anything wrong."

Oh, god, he was in that sort of mood. Teasing. Tormenting.

I bent over the bed. I offered myself to him. He didn't take a step in my direction.

I slid my fingers into the waistband of my panties. I pulled them down my thighs, arched my back, and gazed at him over my shoulder, pleading silently.

Jack stood there, still staring at me.

"Use your belt, Jack." My stomach was in knots. "Please, Jack—"

He held up the belt as if he'd never seen it before. "This belt?"

Christ.

I knew that the longer he made me beg, the more he made me ask for it, the worse the punishment would ultimately be. When he was finally ready, he would not stop until he was done. I knew all of that. And still I begged.

"Jack...Please...."

He took a step toward the bed, but only to brush my hair out of my eyes and then to run his fingertips along the leather collar tight on my throat. He didn't start to punish me yet. He didn't even look close. My pussy tightened. I could feel how wet my lips had become, the silky juices coating the tops of my thighs. Jack reached a hand between my legs, surprising me, and felt for himself. His eyes burned as he removed his damp fingertips and brought them forward for me to lick clean.

"You want me to whip you?" he asked, casually, as

if we were talking about after-dinner drinks. Would you like a cognac? A sherry? A whipping?

"Yes, Sir."

"Good girl," he murmured, nodding, his eyes roving over my body, arms locked in place, panties down to my knees, ass up.

"But we're in a hotel, kid. What if you cry out?"

I hadn't thought about that. I didn't know what to say. Jack did. From his other pocket, he removed a gag. He hadn't used one on me before. And this was serious.

"Open," he demanded, and I parted my lips and let him slide the devious-looking device into place, felt him buckle the thing behind my head.

"See now?" he said. "No one would say I'm not a conscientious boyfriend. You can scream if you have to and nobody will hear you."

I closed my eyes, humbled by the gag. Humiliated. But Jack was in motion.

Belt in hand, finally ready to start.

Chapter Twenty-Seven:
Small World

"You brought black because it makes you feel strong," Jack observed, watching me dress. He was kicking back on the bed, drinking the coffee I'd fetched from the café downstairs and reading the *New York Times*.

I nodded, then looked at my reflection in the mirror. I had on a short black dress with a white collar and cuffs. It looked expensive, but was actually from a thrift store on Melrose Avenue. Black tights and my favorite shiny Mary Janes completed the look.

Jack made a motion with his finger for me to turn around, and I rotated once, so that he could drink in the whole look.

"Nice," he said. "I do prefer you in color, but you look confident. And that's important."

The truth? I was terrified. I'd been both impatiently awaiting and desperately dreading this New York lunch with my editor at a large sex-themed magazine. The man frightened me to the extreme, at least on paper. His edits were direct and to the point, and he brokered no nonsense. He'd been in the business for a quarter of a century and I felt like an inexperienced little kid at the thought of being with him alone, but Jack told me I'd do fine. And that he'd be waiting for me at the hotel when I was finished.

"I don't know," I started, pulling at the hem of the dress. Maybe this look was wrong. Maybe I should have brought a suit. What were writers supposed to look like? I glanced at my travel clock. I had time. I had started getting dressed more than an hour before I even had to leave.

"What about my black jeans and my Harley shirt from Paris?"

Jack started to laugh. "You're crazy." The floor was littered with discarded outfits.

"You haven't watched me dress for something important before," I told him, pawing through the hotel's tiny little cabinet for something else.

"You don't need a different outfit," Jack assured me, setting his coffee down and pushing aside the *Times*. "You need—"

I was caught off guard. I'd been looking at my clothes, standing there in my bra and panties, garters in place, thinking of what else I might try on. Jack had been thinking of other things entirely, and in a flash, I was over his lap and he had scissored one leg over both of mine. Where had he stashed the paddle that was suddenly in his hand, suddenly slamming down against my black-panty-clad ass?

My breath caught as he landed blow after blow on my rear, and then I started to squirm.

"Don't fight me, baby. You don't want to make me upset." His tone was dead serious, and I paid immediate attention. "I'm giving you a little taste of what to expect tonight. You can think about this when your nerves start to jangle. You can think about what I'm going to do to your sweet little ass this evening."

His warm fingers caught the waistband of my panties and slid them down my thighs. He hesitated, as always, observing the bloom of color on my once-pale cheeks. "Ten on the sweet spot," he said, "Count 'em out for me."

I did as he said, not even considering disobeying. I didn't want him to make me cry before my meeting. Not for real.

The pain was intense, but as always, clarifying. I felt my world slide slowly back into place. Jack was right. He knew what I'd needed. When he was done, he stood me up and brushed my hair back, smiling at me. "There," he said. "Much better. Whatever outfit you choose always will look better after a good old-fashioned spanking."

Jack didn't walk me to the cab. He simply kissed me goodbye, let his hand roam down my body to tighten on my ass, and then said, "Don't worry so much about pleasing him, Samantha. Remember, doll. You only have to worry about pleasing one person."

I don't know why, but that thought made me instantly more relaxed.

My editor's office was exactly like I'd imagined—clean lines, no nonsense. But the art on the wall was tongue-in-cheek. Pornography Kills.

I was awed in the man's presence, humbled and shy, but he was gracious. He immediately ushered me out of the building and to a nearby restaurant, where he asked me if I'd like a glass of wine.

"Oh, yes, please." Wine. Wine would be wonderful.

He ordered for the two of us, and I felt my cheeks go red when he chose cranberry juice for himself. I can drink a few shots, yes, but not on an empty stomach. The fact that he was going to be drinking virgin cranberry juice while I grew progressively tipsy on Chardonnay wasn't lost on me.

Over lunch, he described his years on the magazine and shared different sexy stories about people he knew and places he'd visited. We had acquaintances in common—rich people often travel in the same circles, whether they be editors of pornography, lawyers, or art dealers. He knew Jody's writing partner. He knew the brother of one of my parents' good friends. I had understood that Los Angeles was tiny, but at this lunch I realized how small the world truly was.

"Are you in town for the S/M convention?" he asked out of the blue.

My eyes widened. I hadn't known there was such a thing.

"There are classes on flogging, proper use of breath control, coming on command..."

The wine was working through me, but I wondered if Jack knew about this convention. If perhaps he'd always known. Jack had helped me arrange the time for my trip. Was there an ulterior motive to his plans?

"When we get back to the office, I'll give you a brochure," he promised me.

Although he had been authoritative in his edits, in person he strove to put me at ease. This first meeting, my first taste of being courted as a "real" writer, couldn't have gone more smoothly. Back at the office, he handed me two copies of the issue featuring one of my latest stories and then gave me a warm hug. I reminded him of someone he'd known long ago, he told me.

"Say hello to Jack for me," he said at the door before turning and leaving me in the empty hallway, wondering what on earth he could possibly have meant.

Chapter Twenty-Eight:
Everybody Knows

Jack was waiting for me in the hotel bar, sitting off in a corner. I hesitated before approaching, because one of the stunning catsuit-clad waitresses was bent over in front of him, and I wasn't sure if the jealousy I felt was broadcast on my face. When she moved away, heading off to reveal her bountiful cleavage to another lucky patron, I waded through the customers to the corner and sat in the chair opposite him. Thoughtful as always, Jack had already ordered me a drink, and I took a sip of the martini and felt the tension from my meeting start to slip away.

"You look whipped," Jack said softly. Even in the dim light of the bar, his blue eyes had a glow. "Or as if you're going to be whipped."

I took another quick sip of the drink.

"How did it go?"

"I think I did okay." I described the meal for him.

"You didn't eat anything, though, did you?"

When I'm nervous, I have a difficult time actually

remembering to eat the food on my plate. On my first date with Jack, I managed about two bites. He hadn't forgotten.

"No, but I drank a whole glass of wine."

Jack grinned, and his smile broadened when I confessed that my editor had ordered plain juice for himself. "That's an old trick," he said. "I've done the same thing with new hires at our firm. The response is to say, 'What are you having?' or simply 'I'll have what you're having.' And then you're on equal footing."

"The wine helped, though."

"I'll bet it did."

I took a deep breath. "So... did you know about the S/M convention?"

Jack sat back in his chair and regarded me with a curious look. "What do you think?"

"That you knew."

"Give the girl a prize."

I looked down at my hands.

"I thought we'd go on the weekend," Jack explained. "But I don't want you to be worried. I want you to see what there is out there. I want you to be aware."

I thought about what my editor had described, the lessons in flogging, and I wondered how far Jack might make me go. I didn't ask him how he knew my editor. It didn't feel like the appropriate time. With Jack, things were never what they seemed. I already knew that. But I also understood that I'd have to pay closer attention in the future.

After paying for our drinks, Jack led me from the bar. It was early evening now, and the air was still. Jack took me to dinner at one of his favorite restaurants—also long gone now. A little French place where the owners knew him and greeted him warmly. We sat side by side in the quaint little café and he ordered for us, then wrapped one arm around me. I was lulled by his warmth and his strength, and thus caught off guard when he said, "The waiter's watching you."

"What do you mean?"

Jack leaned in closer to my ear. "He's looking at you. Every time he goes by our table. He thinks he's being sly, but..."

As he spoke, I turned my head to look at the waiter he was talking about, a lean, dark-eyed man who immediately made eye contact with me and held my gaze for a beat too long, bringing a fresh heat to my cheeks.

"See?" Jack murmured.

"I didn't do anything—" I started in my defense.

"Ah, Samantha, I didn't say you did." He paused for emphasis. "But I want you to."

I turned to face him. What in the world did he have in mind?

"Enter into a little flirtatious banter with him," Jack said. "With your eyes. You know how to do it. I'm sure you do."

"Come on, Jack."

"Are you disobeying me?"

I went pinker. "No, of course not."

"Then do as I say. I want to see you flirt. I want to know what you look like when you're making eyes at another man."

Each time the waiter brought us a new plate of food, or refilled our wine glasses, or stopped by simply to check our status, I felt his eyes roam over me. Jack had one strong hand on my thigh under the table, and he kept a steady pressure on my leg, squeezing tightly, wanting me to do as he'd requested.

I tried. With Jack right next to me, flirting felt impossible. But I did my best. I shot the dark-haired boy my best coy, up-from-under glances. I felt rusty, but apparently my tricks worked fine. He seemed mesmerized.

When the after-dinner drinks arrived, Jack put his hand on the side of my neck, his fingertips stroking my bare skin. "The bathrooms are upstairs. Go on up. I'm sure he'll follow you."

"Jack?"

"Get him to kiss you."

"Come on, Jack..."

"Get him to kiss you up there. That's all. Nothing more than that. Only a kiss. Then come back to the table and have your drink as if nothing ever happened."

I felt shaky as I made my way through the restaurant and up the tiny stairs to the landing. There was a pay phone next to a mirrored wall, several prints by Toulouse Lautrec, and two bathroom doors. I hesitated in front of the mirror, fixing my hair, when the waiter came upstairs.

I turned to face him, and he looked at me in the same suggestive way as he had all evening. I smiled, shocked at how right Jack had been. The man started to speak, and I somehow knew what he was going to say before I heard the words.

"So sexy..."

I shook my head and took a step forward. It was all I had to do. He took over, pressing me back against the mirrored wall and kissing me. I could feel how hard he was through his black slacks, could smell his aftershave, could feel the start of his evening beard scrape my cheek. He tried to bring his hands up to my breasts, but I grabbed onto them instead and held them at his sides.

Jack said to kiss. That was all.

The feel of this stranger's mouth on mine sent a powerful shock through me. He kissed so differently from Jack. Soft and slow at first, then gradually growing more passionate. I let the pleasure build within me, and then I pulled back and smiled at him. "I can't," I said. "I can't do any more," and I turned and hurried into the ladies' room, intent on fixing my hair, my smudged lipstick. I stared at my reflection in the bathroom mirror and didn't recognize myself. There was a strange look to my eyes. Sadness? Perhaps. But more of the thrill of the hunt.

Jack was waiting impatiently when I came back downstairs. The table was cleared; the bill was gone. We took a cab back to the hotel and he didn't speak a word the whole ride.

I wondered if I had failed. If the test had not been my obedience in this case, but my refusal. Fear flickered through me, and I felt lost until Jack gripped my wrist and led me to the elevators. And suddenly I understood. I had done what he said. To the very last degree. And now he was going to punish me for it.

Chapter Twenty-Nine:
The Kiss

"What did it feel like?" Jack asked me.

"I was nervous."

"Sure, but what did the kiss feel like?"

I closed my eyes, trying to recreate every detail in my mind. "His lips were soft," I started, "and I could tell that he was a smoker, because he had that dark flavor of tobacco." This isn't a bad thing to me. One of my most intense memories is the way Brock's kisses sometimes tasted silver like smoke.

Jack took my wrists in his hands and gently clicked the cool cuffs into place. I was bound face up on the hotel bed, with my ankles spread and attached to the metal frame under the mattress.

"More," he said, pressing me. "Tell me more."

"I could hear the patrons downstairs," I told him, "and I thought about you sipping your drink and waiting for me..."

"You know, I don't believe you kissed him." Jack now

held a flogger in one hand, and he traced the many fine ends along my ribs, tickling me. "I think you pretended to make a call, that you stayed with your back to him, that you didn't even look in his direction. I think you're making all this up to please me."

I took a deep breath, trying to figure out how to prove myself. "He was wearing some spicy cologne," I started, trying again. "His lips were soft and he pressed them firmly to mine, and then slowly parted them and touched my tongue with his."

Jack changed tactics surprisingly, "How do I know you didn't fuck him?"

He'd gone from disbelief that I'd engaged in a simple kiss to certainty that I'd taken off my panties. And I panicked. "I didn't, Jack. God, of course I didn't." What could I say? "You can tell. Touch me there. Come on. You could tell if I'd been with another man."

"Keep describing what happened."

I was off-center now, and desperate. "I gripped his hands and held them to his sides when he tried to touch my breasts. I kissed him, Jack. That was all. Like you told me."

The flogger danced along my body, landing once, sharply, between my legs, but I didn't beg. Didn't cry out.

"I promise, Jack," I said, my eyes wide. "It was only a kiss."

Jack was in motion now, the weapon graceful in his grip, crisscrossing the blows over that most tender skin. I could feel the strokes as they built in intensity. He started strong, yet worked gradually in force until my hips were squirming on the mattress. There was almost no give in the way he'd bound me, but I could raise and lower my body, could beg with the motions of my hips.

I understood why he was punishing me. This time it was for obeying him. I'd never done anything like this before—kissing another man at the request of my boyfriend. Yeah, I'd cheated on Byron, but obviously not with his permission. I thought about the pleasure I'd gotten by meeting my lovers on the sly—by kissing them, by fucking them—and then returning home to Byron. This was nothing like that emotion. I'd kissed the waiter only because Jack had told me to. I would never have looked in the man's direction if not at the request of my boyfriend.

"Would you have fucked him?" The flogger was gone, on the floor, and Jack was bent by my feet, undoing the bindings.

"No, Jack, no!"

"If I'd told you to go upstairs and take off your panties and wait for him, would you have obeyed me?"

Ah, Jesus. It was a trap. I'd fallen in. I'd failed.

"No, Jack…" He was turning me now, arranging me face down on the bed. My pussy throbbed from the flogging, but I knew that pain had been a mere wake-up call to whatever he had planned next.

"You'd have disobeyed me?"

A trick. A cruel Dom trick.

"I don't want to fuck anyone else, Jack."

"But you did want to kiss him?"

I turned my head, looking up at him over my shoulder. I felt helpless, and timid, a rabbit caught in a snare. "Please—"

"Please, what, baby?" He was right next to me, his mouth so close. "Please kiss you? Like you kissed him?"

I was fucked. I got that now. If I'd disobeyed in the restaurant, he would have undoubtedly spanked me right there, in public, as he had threatened to do in the past. I'd had that image in my mind, the thought of him raising my skirt and lowering my panties so that everyone in the restaurant could see my ass, see it get tanned. So I had done what he'd told me. But if he had ordered me to fuck the waiter, I would not have obeyed. I'd have begged him, pleaded. I would have done whatever he had said in order to please him in a different manner. There was a line I was unwilling to cross. Jack was illuminating that line for me.

"Slut," Jack said under his breath, standing once more. I watched him undo his belt. I waited for him to strike. Instead, he brought the cold metal buckle up to my lips. He waited for me to kiss it. The concept of kissing now felt tainted. "I'm not going to give you the gag tonight," Jack said sadly. "You're going to have to keep yourself quiet."

He took his time. The buckle caught my skin every few blows, and I knew those bruises were going to last. They would be the ones to turn dark blue and purple. The ones to hurt when I sat. I cried, tears streaking my face, wetting the pillow. But I did not scream. I did not fight.

I had failed him.

By obeying, I had failed.

I deserved whatever he had to give me.

I was sure he would leave me tied all night. That he wouldn't fuck me. That he might even leave the room, leave me alone in my misery. I prepared myself for that concept, hoping that I would behave in a manner that would please him. That I would not let him down twice in one night. So when he stripped off his clothes, I was surprised.

* * *

Jack left me tied. I had that part right. And he spit on his fingertips and worked that wetness around my hole. He fucked me as hard as he'd whipped me, taking my ass with an almost frightening intensity.

When he was done, he still kept me tied, but he didn't leave the room. He wrapped his body around mine and held me like that, his warmth embracing me, soothing me.

"You can't always win," he whispered.

I stayed silent.

"There was no way tonight for you to win. It was a losing proposition from the start." He lifted my dark hair off my neck and blew his breath against me.

I thought of my college roommate's print of The Kiss on the wall of my college dorm. I thought of Deena cooing about the sexiness of the image, how it would be so divine to have a man kiss you like that. And I turned my head and met Jack's ice-blue eyes as he finally kissed me for the first time that night. Really kissed me.

Divine.

Chapter Thirty:
A Day of Firsts

I met with my publisher the next day. And although I remember what I wore—yes, it was all black—and how well I was received, the meeting itself has become a blur. The publisher treated me extremely graciously. As a first-time author, I was in awe. I wish I could describe our conversation, or tell you how witty I was, but all I know is that I turned in my manuscript, shook the hand of my editor, and at some point found myself back out on the street.

My next appointment was with the managing editor at another sex magazine, and I remember this one much more clearly. My editor was luscious, perfectly suited for the lighthearted environment. She had a tiny office filled with an assortment of hilariously vulgar sex toys (the Tongue!), pin-up pictures of bare-chested men, sparkling rhinestone tiaras, dried flowers, and other girly items. She was loud and funny and introduced me around the office as if I were a celebrity.

And then she did something totally unexpected. She took me to another floor in the same building to have me meet the publisher of a line of erotic books. The book line was owned by the same company as the magazine, and she thought I might find a nice niche here.

I will say honestly that the publisher—I'll call him JR—was less than interested. He thought that if I wrote for her magazine, I'd be far too soft-core for his world. I told him about my upcoming book, and after listening to me describe a few of the more S/M-style scenes, he agreed to give me a try. I was to sketch an outline for a Victorian-themed novel, and send it to him when I got back home. (I didn't have an exclusive contract with my first publishing house.)

By the end of the day, I felt shell-shocked. But more importantly, I felt like a writer. A real writer.

Jack didn't care how I felt. I don't think he'd have treated me any differently if I were a popcorn girl or a truck-stop waitress. Jack didn't really care what I did. He only cared about who I was. Kindly, he let me crash on the bed for a few minutes while he shaved. During the afternoon, he'd bought several different bottles of liquor, and they stood on the windowsill.

I was sipping a glass of whiskey, my shoes off, pillows piled behind my head, when Jack re-entered the room. He stood there for a moment, looking at me. He had on a pair of slacks but no shirt, and I gazed back at him, admiring his flat stomach and the taut muscles of his arms.

"Take off your clothes."

I'd been waiting for him to pay attention to me, and I was more than ready to obey. I slid off the short black skirt and black silky T-shirt, then pulled off my tights.

"Bra and panties, too."

These were both black as well, and I took them off and tossed them into the corner. Jack left me alone for a minute, then came toward the bed with his razor, cream, and a cup of water. He sat the implements on the bedside table, then returned to the bathroom, re-emerging with one of the hotel's folded fluffy white towels.

"Lift your hips."

He placed the towel beneath me, and then started to spread the shaving cream over my pussy lips. I keep myself neat and trim at all times, but Jack spread the cream all over the entire region of my sex, and I understood that he was going to shave me bare.

Jack worked quickly, without any apparent fear. He slicked the razor over my skin, then dipped the blade in the glass of warm water. He moved my legs wider apart when he needed to and used his fingers to pinch my lips, maneuvering me exactly how he wanted.

When he was finished, he brought me into the shower and had me wash away the shaving cream Then he said, "Sit on the edge of the tub and spread your legs."

I obeyed immediately. Jack bent on his knees in front of me, and he used his tongue to make sure he had performed the job well. I was entirely bare, completely clean. Jack tricked his tongue over me, until I had to grip onto his shoulders to keep myself steady. I felt as if I were floating, lost in the pleasure, until he stopped, abruptly, and led me back into the room.

"Your outfit is in the top drawer," he said. "Be ready when I get out of the shower."

My legs were weak. He had almost brought me off with his tongue. But I should have known that there would be more to his plan. Jack never stopped at the expected. He always took an encounter further than I could envision. I opened the drawer to find a red plastic bag with the edge sealed over. I carried the bag to the bed and sat down, nerves electrified. The bag didn't seem all that big. Not big enough to hold an entire outfit. But it was. Inside the bag I found a black vinyl dress with a silver zipper that ran its length. One tug and the wearer would be entirely revealed. I wondered if I should put on a bra and panties beneath the dress. But Jack hadn't said to, and there were none in the bag.

Quickly, I slid into the dress and pulled the zipper. Jack knew me so well. The glossy material fit my body perfectly. I ran my hands over the shiny surface, then returned on a whim to the drawer. Yes, at the very back was a pair of shoes. High spike-heeled shoes. I was sitting on the edge of the bed working the buckle on the ankle when Jack came out of the bathroom. He had a white towel around his waist, and he looked as desirable as he always did.

"Stand up," he said.

I did my best, tottering in the heels.

"Turn for me."

I spun around.

"Lovely. Now lie down on the bed while I get ready."

Moving was difficult. The dress was so tight. But I scooted back on the mattress, leaning on the pillows once more. Jack bent down and looked up the line of my body, and I knew he was gazing up under the hem to make sure I hadn't snuck on a pair of underwear.

"Good girl," he said as he got his own clothes on. "Lift your dress for me."

With effort, I slid the hem up past my thighs to my waist. Now, Jack had on his black slacks and a black short-sleeved T-shirt. He came to my side, parted my freshly shaved pussy lips, and let me see the silvery clip in his hand before he clamped it to my clit. He was a true magician. I bucked immediately, but Jack shook his head.

"Behave," he warned. "You take it."

I nodded, that first spark of pain rushing through me before slowly subsiding.

"It's going to be a long night, baby," Jack said, and he pulled a collar from the bedside table and motioned for me to sit. I felt him fasten the buckle into place tight on my neck, but not too tight. "And I want you to make me proud." The leash that dangled in his hand sent panic through me. Was he going to lead me through the lobby like an animal? I couldn't fathom that. Nothing we had done so far had prepared me for this sort of endeavor. "Jack," I started, the words coming before I could think to stop them. Before I could quiet my inner worries. "Wait..."

"Ah, baby," Jack murmured sadly, and almost before I knew what was happening, I was ass-up over his lap, in what I could only think of now as a standard position for me. Was there a day when Jack didn't give me an over-the-knee spanking? I didn't think so. I couldn't remember one. "I thought I'd get to deliver your first spanking of the evening when we got there, Samantha. But I guess you need a little taste before we go."

His hand came down hard and fast, no gentle warm-up, no sweet caressing of my curves. The pain was instantaneous as always, but all I could think of were the words: *When we got there.*

Where?

Where were we going?

I could only imagine.

Chapter Thirty-One:
Love Is the Drug

The sleek leather collar had a silver loop at the front, and I fully expected Jack to clip on the leash and walk me down the hallway toward the elevator like some trained pet on display. I felt a wave of fear at the thought. What would he do to me? Would he make me crawl on my hands and knees? Would he smack me with the doubled-up leash if I misbehaved? He hadn't played with me like this before, and fear nearly paralyzed me.

I thought of begging, of telling him I'd do whatever he wanted within the confines of our room if he would only put that leash away. But that was silly. He knew I'd do whatever he wanted. I had no bargaining power, no tricks down my garters. No garters at all.

Still, I thought of trying, of bending over the bed, spreading my cheeks, of asking him to fuck my ass. Jack loved when I asked for this, when I begged for it. That turned him on like almost nothing else. Nothing except when I asked him to whip me. When the need overflowed, spilled from my lips, Jack basked in my begging. Somehow I could tell that he had his mind made up. There was nothing I would be able to do to alter the course of the evening.

This is why I was surprised when he took pity on me. Pity Jack-style, that is. After spanking me until my ass felt neon-red, he stood me up and flicked the clamp off my clit with a casual gesture of his fingers. Then he grabbed me by the shoulders and pushed me toward the corner of the room, and I understood immediately. I'd been naughty. I was to face the corner. My dress still hiked to my hips, scarlet cheeks on display for him.

Listening to Jack getting ready wound my nerves even tighter. I didn't dare look at him, and I couldn't fathom what he was doing from the sounds of the motions. And then finally I got it. He'd poured himself a drink and was relaxing on the bed. Reading the paper? Maybe. Or perhaps looking for something in the paper. Was he taking me out to a show dressed like this? My heart thudded. How long would he make me stand here? The shoes were crazy-high, and I had to work to stand straight and tall, focused intently on how every part of my body felt. My ass throbbed. The thin leather bands of the shoes cut into my ankles. My pussy...

"Turn around," Jack said suddenly.

I did what he said.

"Fix your dress."

My fingers fumbled as I pulled the fabric back into place. Jack tilted his head at me, taking in my entire outfit. Then he came forward and lowered the zipper on the dress in the front, giving him access to my breasts.

"Offer them to me," he said. "Hold them out."

I lifted my breasts for him, and he quickly fastened

a clip onto each one, letting the cool silver chain dangle between them. When he zipped the dress back up for me, I looked down. I could easily see the outline of the nipple clamps and the chain pressed against the vinyl dress. Shame floored me. If I could see the clamps, then anyone could.

"Perfect," Jack murmured, as if the final touch was all I needed to make myself presentable. He grinned at me, that half-smile so disarming that for one moment, I felt my worries disappear. And then flare right back up again as I watched him slide the leash into his pocket, then motion for me to follow him. My heart was beating so fast that I was sure he could hear the rhythm of it. Maybe that's the sound he decided to fuck me to. Because as soon as we got into the elevator, the one with the hellish-red light glowing overhead, Jack pressed the UP button and pushed me toward the wall. My hands went up automatically, bracing myself as Jack worked my form-fitting dress back to my hips. That dress was definitely getting one hell of a workout.

"I love the way your ass looks after a spanking," he told me. "So sweet and cherry." He stroked my hot skin and then leaned forward. I could feel his cock against me, pressing. Was he really going to fuck me in the elevator?

That's easy to answer: Yes.

I didn't say a word, didn't beg or plead. I had an inkling that tonight would be full of surprises, and I could read Jack's moods fairly well already by now. He was waiting for me to make a false move, to give him one reason to take me to my limits. The spanking had been a warning, a quick and powerful way to let me know not to mess with him, not to disobey. But I didn't want to disobey. I'd been dying to have him take me ever since he'd shaved me bare.

His cock slid inside me easily. As usual, the spanking had made me wetter than I wanted to admit. How could it be punishment if my pussy responded with such immediate pleasure? Jack didn't say a word about how turned on I was. He fucked me, as fiercely as I could take, one hand hovering near the row of buttons, so that the elevator shot up to the top floor, then back down to the middle.

I wondered what Jack would do if someone chose to get on. I could see it in my head, a shocked patron watching the doors slide open, seeing Jack thrusting into me, seeing the red light coloring my already crimson ass.

"You like that," Jack said, as if reading my mind.

"Yes. Yes, Sir."

"The thought that someone might see you."

"Yes, Sir," I told him.

"Don't worry, baby. Plenty of people are going to see you tonight."

My body responded instantly, my inner muscles clenching down on him. People, I thought. People are going to be seeing me. Jack brought one hand up into my hair, pulling my head back. "God, you're tight," he moaned. "So fucking tight."

I don't know how long he worked me, I only know he didn't come. He simply pulled my hips back forcefully against him, sealing our bodies together, as the elevator made the final true descent to the lobby.

"Good girl," Jack said, when I remained silent. My eyes were squeezed shut, and I was certain we'd get caught. But I would not beg him to pull out. I would not give him a reason to spank me in the lobby. I had a vision of him doing exactly that. Sitting down on one of those velvety lounges and thrashing my still-throbbing ass with the cruel leather of his belt. Would we be arrested for that? Or did patrons at the upscale hotel find this sort of X-rated display amusing, entertaining even?

As my mind raced, the doors slid open—but we escaped unscathed, Jack pulling out and tucking himself back into his slacks before anyone could see us. He kindly blocked my body with his, readjusting my dress one more time for me, and then led me out of the elevator and into the ultra-chic lobby. I was shaky on those heels, anyway—more so now, so freshly fucked—but I realized as Jack held me around the waist and herded me toward the outer doors that he hadn't walked me on a leash. He hadn't made me follow on all fours. He had been kind, had taken pity on me in his own way.

I don't know Manhattan well. Once, when I was younger, I got turned around and headed nearly ten blocks in the wrong direction before a kind shopkeeper told me that the Empire State Building—where I was supposed to meet my friends—was the other way.

So I don't know where Jack instructed the cab driver to take us. I only know that once we were whizzing in the right direction, Jack gripped the back of my head and pulled me down to his lap.

His zipper was open. My lips were wet.

I knew what to do.

Chapter Thirty-Two:
Safe

When we got to the club, Jack paid the cab driver, but he didn't lead me to the front door. Instead, he ushered me around the corner, into the mouth of a dark alley, and pulled something unexpected out of his pocket.

"Put these on."

They were panties, ruffled black satin panties with full coverage, front and rear. I didn't understand, but I didn't hesitate. Jack held me steady while I stepped into the knickers and slid them up under that tightest of dresses. I don't know why I was always so many steps behind Jack, why I could never see the full picture. Because as soon as we entered the club, he herded me to a "coat check" corner, unzipped my dress with one quick tug, and handed the sleek sheath to the pretty dreadlocked woman running the booth.

I'd thought the panties were to make me feel more comfortable, less exposed. In a way, they were. I'd probably have hidden under a chair if Jack had made me walk around entirely naked. But I wasn't far from it. I crossed my hands over my breasts, and Jack pulled my hands down to my sides and relieved me of the nipple clamps while that pretty girl watched. Then he handed over a bra that matched the panties.

It was as if I were in one of those dreams, where you find yourself naked in a store window, and people point at you and stare. No, I wasn't naked, but the bra and panty set didn't provide me nearly as much coverage as I would have liked.

"You'll feel better like this, won't you?" he asked, as if he only had my best interests at heart.

Before I could answer Jack, he had moved on, now fastening that hateful leash to my collar, giving the coat check—dress check?—girl a wink, and dragging me along on those tottering heels behind him.

The crowd was made up of a mélange of hipsters. Mostly young, mostly dressed in dark colors, all looking as if you could cast them in an ad for some cool new vodka. When I looked around the room, I saw that Jack was the most out of place. He was older than many of the patrons by a good two decades, and he had on simple, expensive black attire. No rubber or vinyl or netting for Jack. But he moved as if he owned the place, his confidence so obvious, so attractive, that I knew that when people stared at him, it was in awe or lust, not condescension. He let the leash hang between the two of us, not keeping me tight at his side, but I worked to stay close by. I didn't want to be caught up, twisted around other people.

I wanted to be next to my man.

Jack didn't spare me a glance; he simply led me through the crowd to a corner of the room where a long, leather bench ran the length in both directions. I didn't have to be told not to sit at his side. I sat on the floor, my knees beneath me, my back arched, and Jack put one hand on my head, kindly stroking my hair as if I truly had become his pet.

The music was loud, as it had been in the club with Nathan, and the room was warm from all the dancing bodies. But as I looked around, I felt that I fit in. There were others in attire (or lack of attire) similar to my own. I saw collars and cuffs and a variety of toys on display. I actually started to relax.

Jack was hardwired into my emotions. How else would he know to act as soon as I began to feel comfortable? How else would he understand exactly when to strike in order to keep me off balance?

He bent down to whisper into my ear, "Choose your safeword."

This wasn't anything we'd talked about before. Jack read me so well that I put my trust totally in him. I didn't ever think I'd want him to stop before he was ready. "It can't be 'No,'" he continued, "because sometimes 'No' doesn't mean 'No.'"

I nodded.

"It can't be 'Please,' or 'Stop,' or anything that might come to your lips accidentally. You have to think of a special word, and then you have to tell it…"

I thought he was going to say "to him." What other words would complete that sentence? But Jack was different. Jack was always three long strides ahead of me.

"You have to tell it to him."

Jack motioned to a man standing nearby. Someone I hadn't even noticed yet, my eyes busy roaming the crowd, looking for like-minded subs. This man was dressed in the part of the Dom. Leather pants. Tight black shirt. And a crop in one hand. Did he know Jack? Were they friends? My mind raced faster than ever, whirling with possibilities. Jack owned a place in New York. I knew that. But I hadn't considered that might mean he was a regular at clubs like this, clubs that catered to the darkest of sexual fantasies.

"Go on, now," Jack hissed, tossing the handle of the leash to the man. "Make sure you tell him, Sam. He won't stop otherwise."

Oh god...oh, my fucking god...Had I thought Jack was kind for giving me panties to wear? Had I thought he was considerate for taking off those painful clamps and providing me with a bra? There was nothing kind in his blue eyes now. There was nothing considerate at all in his expression. It was as if he were a stranger.

The man tugged on the leash and I felt my heart stop. The collar was pulled tight on my neck, and I had no choice but to stand and follow or be dragged along behind. But dragged where? I turned my head, looking at Jack, pleading with my eyes, and felt a fresh wave of ice-cold panic when I realized he wasn't even paying attention. Was he not going with me? Was he not going to come?

I wondered suddenly if this was another test. I understood now that I should have refused to kiss the waiter. I'd learned that much. Should I now refuse to let this man, this Dom, whip me, even if that was what Jack wanted?

I tugged back on the leash, using both hands, and the Dom stopped and turned, and I saw a smile on his face that I was entirely unprepared for. He came close and bent down low. "Spunk," he said, "I like that. So many subs come along willingly, no heart at all." His grip was like iron as he brought my wrists down from the leash and captured them easily behind my back. I was wrong to think that Jack wasn't paying attention, because there he was behind me, locking my wrists into place, making the concept of struggling that much more difficult.

Still, I wasn't ready. I pressed back against Jack, pushing my body into his. I turned my head to look over my shoulder, meeting his eyes.

"Go, Samantha. Follow him." His expression was stern.

"I will," I said, my voice shaking, "If you want me to. But I need to know..."

He put up a hand, stopping the Dom from moving, and he turned me around to face him.

"You need to know what?"

I didn't know how to phrase it. If this were a test, then I should be smart enough to figure it out myself. But was the test whether I would let another man punish me? Or was it whether I'd refuse, dig in my heels, and let all hell break loose? My heart sank. I couldn't read Jack's eyes. In total desperation, I went on my knees once more, not knowing what else to do. I wanted to curl up into a ball. I wanted to have a safeword to say to Jack so that he would let me know the answers to all my questions. To my undeniable relief, Jack bent down with me, in order to hear my voice, begging now, unsure, scared.

"Please, Jack..."

He stroked my hair. He lifted my chin.

"Are you disobeying me?" His eyes were warm now, but his voice was cold.

I shook my head.

"Go with him. I want to see what you look like when another man whips you. I want to watch. Do you understand that?"

I nodded.

"Will you do this for me?"

I nodded again and let myself be brought back to standing, let the man lead me to another room, understanding that Jack would be close by. That I would be safe. And that this was what he desired.

It was all I needed to know.

Jack followed after us. I was secure in the knowledge of his proximity. Maybe he would punish me later for this scene that was about to play out, but not because I had failed a test. Simply because punishing me made Jack hard.

The Dom never told me his name. He bound me in place in one of the back rooms, and then instructed me to address him as Master.

"Do you understand?"

"Yes, Master." It sounded phony to me. A game. A play. Jack was Sir. No doubt. No hesitation. Yet I obeyed, for Jack.

"Your safeword."

I'd been trying, working, to come up with something that would make sense. I understood what Jack had told me. Not *No, Stop, Don't,* or *Please.* Still, it had to be a word that I could actually make myself say, not something silly, that would add to the oddness of this encounter. Not aardvark or tomato or Aerosmith.

"Uncle," I ultimately whispered, remembering playing rough and tumble with my cousins every summer, torturing one another until one would finally call Uncle. That seemed okay to me, and the man, who might have had similar experiences in his youth, gave me an accepting nod.

"You are to thank me after each stroke."

"Yes, Master."

He moved to stand behind me, and fear flashed through

me once more. The sound level in the place became white noise, a background melody. I could only guess that this man was making me wait in order to further ratchet up my level of total insecurity. But then I saw, in a mirror on the wall, that he was talking to Jack. My own cruel man came forward, and with a flash of silver, my panties were cut from my body. I closed my eyes, and tried to find that place within myself where I can make everything all right. That safe place.

There was no word of warning before the whipping started There was only the sound of my heart in my ears, and the sensation of the crop meeting my skin. And then Jack in front of me, pushing my hair from my face, staring at me, drinking in every emotion that flared through my dark brown eyes.

I flinched at the blows, my body tightening, then working to relax. "Thank you, Master." I choked out. Every time. Brock and I had played a similar game way back when. Brock had liked to hear me thank him each time he brought his belt against my ass. So I was trained already, the only differences being the public quality of the location and the fact that it was a stranger cropping my naked skin and not someone who loved me.

But Jack wasn't a stranger. Jack was in front of me, watching me, and his closeness gave me strength.

"Thank you, Master." I spoke the words over and over again, thanking this dark Dom for hurting me, for giving me the pain that both Jack and I craved.

The Dom didn't ask me to count. I don't know how many stripes I took. I felt as if I were hovering above myself, free from the pain, watching from above. But finally, Jack gripped my face between both hands and whispered, "He won't stop, kid. He's like a machine. If you think you're going to outlast him, you're wrong."

I've always been the kind of person to take a dare, always the one who needs to prove my strength. In school, during those insane nationally sponsored physical-fitness tests, where the teachers had us hang from monkey bars while they timed us, I outlasted everyone by minutes, rather than seconds, hanging on until the teachers said to let go. I'm built small, but tough. And I felt as if I would be letting Jack down by giving in, even as the tears started to streak my cheeks, even as the skin on my ass and upper thighs began to throb, to shriek in protest.

"Say it, kid," Jack urged, and I met his eyes, and said, "Thank you, Master."

"Say it, Samantha," Jack demanded, as the Dom behind me struck again. I sensed we had a small crowd around us now, but I didn't turn my head away, didn't even lift my eyes to the mirror to see.

The crop struck another blow. "Thank you, Master," I murmured.

"Christ, Sam, tell him your safeword." Jack didn't know my safeword, and somehow this gave me a tiny spark of power. Was I topping from below? Had I gone over the edge? Jack had brought me here to teach me something, and clearly I was failing to learn the lesson at hand.

The crop sliced through the air. "Thank you, Master," I parroted, my face glistening from the tears now, my voice barely audible. And then Jack did something that made me wetter than I've ever been. He moved his body to shield my own, covering me up with his own skin. I could feel his arms tight around me, his mouth against my ear. "Say it," he insisted, and then his body tightened, and I understood that the Dom—not seeming to care who the fuck he cropped—had let a blow land on Jack's body. And then another. And another. Jack didn't flinch, didn't say a word to me now, he simply protected me.

And I couldn't stand that.

"Uncle," I said, loud enough, and the Dom dropped his weapon and Jack moved aside so that I could be released from the bindings. Jack took off his shirt and pulled it over my nearly naked body, then carried me through the crowd and out to the front of the club. Somehow, he slid me back into my dress. Somehow, he got us a cab, and I found myself curled in his arms, safe once more. Safe at last.

Chapter Thirty-Three:
Shine On, You Crazy Diamond

He took me back to the hotel that night, and he didn't say a word during the whole cab ride or the trip up in the elevator—the purple one this time. He didn't say I'd done well, didn't say I'd failed him. I couldn't tell his thoughts in any way by the manner in which he treated me. I felt meek, cowed, as he drew a bath for me in the cool ceramic tub and lit candles, tiny tea lights that I had bought on a whim. I am the type of person who believes food tastes better on a pretty plate. That atmosphere is almost as important as the main event. I've always been a fan of wearing sexy panties even if there's no one there to see them—or in Jack's case, no one there to cut them off. Jack understood this from the start.

He washed me in the tub and then let me relax alone. I heard him in the adjoining room, but I didn't even try to make sense of the noises. Finally, Jack came back, right as the water was starting to cool, and lifted me up, dried me off, wrapped me in a fresh towel, and led me back to the bedroom.

"Oh, god, Jack," I whispered, hand going to my mouth, towel falling from my body. "I can't..."

I was limp with release more than exhaustion, and I hadn't thought of what the scene might have done to Jack. What he might want afterwards. What he might need.

But to paraphrase that famous Tom Cruise flick, Jack was on me from "I can't"—this wasn't an acceptable response, and we both knew it. Jack had a brand-new set of restraints on the bed, and he fastened them to my body quickly, leather ones that buckled on my wrists, then attached neatly to a set on my upper thighs. I couldn't raise my arms up, couldn't hide or protect myself in any way. But the restraints were not what had caused me alarm.

There were toys lined up neatly on the bedside table. Plugs in various sizes. A bottle of lube.

I didn't say a word now, scared of betraying myself with my voice. I didn't think I could take another scene like the one in the club. Jack bent me over on the bed, pillows under my hips to raise them, and then slicked the lube between the cheeks of my ass. I turned my head away, feeling raw and used already, as Jack slid the smallest plug inside me.

Shame floored me, as it always did when Jack played like this. Yes, I had begged Byron to fuck my ass, but it would have been completely different with him, something dirty we were engaging in together. With Jack, there was the sense of being willingly violated, the way his hands were rough on me, spreading me. The way he held me open and stared down at me, inspecting me.

When the first plug was in place, he flipped me over on the mattress and bent down between my legs. His tongue on my clit was the last thing I expected. The reward of the experience confused my brain even more. He licked me forcefully, his tongue running up and down between my pussy lips, and then he made those dangerous circles around my clit, until I was breathless with yearning. And only then did he turn me back over, unceremoniously pull that plug out, and move on to the next size up.

I understood what he was doing. He was showing me that I was his. That he was in control of my pleasure, of my embarrassment, of my very sense of self. He needn't have worried. I knew I was his. I had known from the start. It didn't matter to me that someone else had just cropped me. As far as I was concerned, that man was a tool, like Jack said: a machine.

He had to work harder to slide the second plug inside of me, and I bit into my bottom lip and pressed my face against the rumpled white sheets. I didn't whine or complain when his hands touched my welts, when white-hot pain flared through me, leaving me shaking. The pain stabilized me, as always, gave me something to hold on to.

Jack repositioned me onto my back once more, and for a moment I was extremely aware of the size of the plug in my ass. The feeling of being stretched was overwhelming. That is, at least, until Jack resumed his place between my forcefully spread thighs and lapped at my throbbing clit once more. I wished my hands were free so I could stroke his hair, touch his face. Jack pushed my thighs wide, and I shut my eyes and felt him licking from the base of my pussy up to my pubic bone. The pleasure that traveled through my body made me dizzy. But when he lifted up and spoke, the pleasure built rather than subsided at the words he said.

"I wanted to do that at the club," he said. "I wanted to

go on my knees in front of you while he was whipping you and lick your sweet pussy."

The image was almost too sexy to stand.

"Make you come while you were being cropped. That's what I wanted to do... But I couldn't stop watching you, watching your face, and then I understood somehow that you weren't going to give your word. God, Sam, why?"

I shrugged. How could I explain it?

"You would have passed out before you spoke, wouldn't you?"

I couldn't meet his eyes now. What did he want from me? Saying the word would have been losing, failing.

Failing Jack and myself.

He was flipping me over once more, and my heart sank at the size of the last plug waiting on the nightstand. But when Jack slid out the second toy, he didn't reach for the third. Instead, I felt warm skin on me, Jack's body on mine, and then his cock inside my ass. He couldn't wait. He talked to me as he fucked me, knees pushing my thighs wide apart, hands stroking over the welts on my skin.

"I wanted to film it," he said, his cock thrusting so hard. "To film him whipping you, and then make you watch the movie later. Make you watch yourself while I whipped you. We'll do that, Samantha. You and me." In and out, his hands now spanking me, my thighs, my ass, as he fucked me, as if he couldn't help himself. But as always when Jack took my ass, everything else faded away. I could hear the sounds of the smacks on my skin, but I could no longer feel them.

"Force you to watch," he said, "while I took you further. He'd use the crop. I'd choose a cane."

My pussy tightened, and when Jack spoke again, I heard the dark smile in his voice. Without saying a word,

I'd told him what I thought of that image. Even though the concept of being filmed was beyond frightening to me, the way Jack presented the scene turned me on.

"You lit up the place," Jack whispered, and I could tell he was reaching his limits.

I was going to come. I could feel it.

"The way you took the pain," Jack continued, almost sounding awed. "The way you absorbed each blow. You shone—" he gripped my thick hair, making me arch, making me look back at him. "There's no other way to describe it."

Pounding into me, slamming into me.

"And I didn't want him to stop." It was like Jack was confessing now, telling me secrets. "I didn't want the whipping to end." His words coming as fast as his thrusts. "But he had to stop." I was coming, those tremors of pure pleasure shaking me, shaking Jack. "You wouldn't tell him. You wouldn't give your word."

I saw Jack in my head, blocking me, shielding me, and I felt his body collapse on mine as he came inside me.

"You shone," he murmured, gripping me up in his strong embrace, sealing me to him, even bound as I was.

It's a sad song, you know.

It always makes me cry.

Chapter Thirty–Four:
Cherry Red

We flew to Los Angeles together, like a real couple, and when Jack drove us back to his place on Sunset, it felt like a real home.

But a truly sterile home.

Jack didn't have anything personal on display. There were no framed photos of his friends, his family, his dog. No postcards pinned to the bulletin board in the office. No silly cartoons taped to his fridge. Jack's style went beyond minimalist to spartan, which I'll admit is the opposite of my magpie-like tendency to collect and display treasures.

I had bowed to Byron's style, as I had no money to change the miserable surroundings. We'd ended up with places designed by his mother, who fancied herself a self-taught interior decorator. And so the rooms all had a Nagel-esque eighties feel, with gray carpets, pink accents, and oddly shaped stuffed dolls sitting lazily in ceramic chairs atop all the shelves. Neither of our living quarters (the triplex near Fairfax, the townhouse in Santa Monica) ever felt truly like home to me, or even like a place I'd choose to live.

But Jack's was different. It was a bare canvas. He didn't even have coffee table books out, or magazines, or reading material on his bedside table. Most pieces of furniture were black or white. All were clearly expensive. Solid. Well made. Nothing flimsy or delicate.

Jack picked up his routine immediately, and I continued my leave of absence from the salon while I prepared my Victorian outline for my new publisher. But my work habits are non-traditional, and I had plenty of time on my own. Time to shop for flowers. For candles. For delicate plates that didn't match and wine glasses with colored stems. Jack didn't say anything until he found me one evening reading in bed under a scarlet blanket. His sheets were white, the comforters white or black. I'd added a striking element to the room, one he couldn't ignore.

He didn't speak right away. He sat on the edge of the bed, then ran his fingers over the blanket's hem. It was cozy, something to wrap up in on a crisp fall day. And it was blood red. I met his eyes and waited. Jack handled everything: paid for the restaurants, the gas for the cars, the food in the fridge. He was in control of nearly all aspects of our world, and now I'd brought color to his room. I wondered if he'd noticed the flowers on his dresser. They were as bright as the blanket, velvety roses that I'd arranged in a simple black-and-white vase. I wasn't trying to remake Jack. I was only trying to colorize him.

"Pretty," he said finally. He had a glass in his hand, as always after work. A single shot of scotch tonight.

I grinned. "Me or the blanket?"

"You."

"But what do you think of the blanket?"

He shrugged. "I don't really see my surroundings all that much," he admitted. "I've always been more into the mental than the physical." I understood what he meant. Sometimes I'd see him on the couch and think he was sleeping, but he'd be pondering some aspect of a case he was working on. Gone from the physical world. Lost to me until he pulled himself back. I'd learned by now not to disturb him at times like this; it would be like waking a bear from deep hibernation.

I pushed on. "But the flowers, the candles in the bathroom, the books on the coffee table." I'd bought them at my favorite bookstore on Sunset, selecting black-and-white photography books. Not trying to crash Jack's world to the ground, simply to enhance it. I'd been an art history major at school. I knew which books to choose.

"You're all the color I need," Jack said, coming closer, setting his drink down on the nightstand. "You seem to blend in at first, dark hair, pale skin, perfect for my black and white environment. But then you change."

"What do you mean?"

"Your cheeks turn pink when I make you blush. Your lips become a dark berry color when you bite them, nervous, wondering what I'm going to do to you next. Your ass, after I spank you, takes on that wonderful shade of well-punished red."

I squeezed my eyes shut tight. I'd been hoping to get a rise out of him, and clearly I had. But the way he was talking, and moving, poetic and slow, had me off balance. Sometimes when Jack was on his way home from work, he'd call and give me a chore or an assignment, letting me know what was in store for me. "Get out the crop." "Put on your collar." Other times he'd burst through the door with electric energy and take me into the hallway or out on the balcony. But this was different. He was moving slowly, like a panther stalking its prey, and I felt mesmerized, at his mercy.

"Look at me."

I couldn't disobey. I opened my eyes, wrapping my arms tight around my body under that blanket. It felt silly now to have bought the thing. So noticeable in this stark black and white world. What was I trying to prove?

"How did you think I'd respond to your changes? Did you think I'd be angry?"

I shrugged. "I didn't know."

"Or pleased?"

I shrugged again. I'd known he would have a reaction, but I wasn't sure what it would be.

"Did you think I'd kick you out for buying dishes that don't match?" He was looking at me directly as he spoke, and he didn't wait for my answer. "You're testing your boundaries," Jack grinned. "Like a child. You want to see if you push this far, what will happen. If you're late to a meeting, will I break up with you, or merely spank your ass until you can't sit down? You're on a quest." He was still smiling, and that made me breathe easier. "Which is understandable. This is a whole new world for you, isn't it?"

"Yes, Jack." I wondered if he was right. Was I testing my limits? Was that what I was doing?

"Truth?" he asked. "I don't really care. I wouldn't see it if you painted the floor blue, if you hung naked pictures on the wall, if you decorated the kitchen in cherry-print paper." He took a breath, then clarified, "I mean, I'd see it, of course, but I wouldn't. It wouldn't matter. Yes, I like things orderly, but that's because I've lived alone for so long, and it's easier if there isn't much stuff to fuck around with. But if you want a red blanket, you can have a red blanket. If you want roses, you can have roses. I'm not trying to be callous. I don't care. What's important to me is that, at the end of the day, I get to do this."

I'd been waiting. I knew there would be a moment when he would strike. But he'd lulled me, soothed me with his deep, sexy voice, and when the moment came, I was unprepared. Jack pulled the blanket away with an unexpected flourish, and then he paused. I'd had the blanket up to my neck as if I were cold. He didn't know I was naked underneath.

"That makes things easier, doesn't it?" he murmured, and I found myself hauled over his lap, his slacks rough on my naked skin, knee pressing up against my sex. He started to spank me, working slowly, methodically, slapping his open palm against my right cheek, then my left. He had a rhythm to his movements, building the intensity of the blows as they grew gradually faster, until he reached across me and snagged a paddle from the top drawer of the bedside table. It was shaped like a Ping-Pong paddle, smooth on one side and rough like sandpaper on the other, and that was the side he used, again and again, winning tears within moments as he punished me. Not for an infraction or for failing in any way. Punished me because he wanted to. Because he could. Because that's what Jack did.

I had a feeling that his goal tonight was to make my ass as deeply scarlet as the blanket. I thought about how I'd felt when I'd bought the thing, wandering the stores on La Brea, choosing this one because of the softness and the hue. Reminding me of the line in the Stones song.

Jack smacked my ass until his arm must have started to ache, and then pushed me onto the bed on top of that brand-new blanket and fucked me. Truly fucked me.

I stared at the roses on the dresser as his cock thrust inside of me, watching as one lone petal dropped to the polished black surface. Jack reached one hand under my body and let his fingertips find my clit, using the weight of my own body to bring me to climax, waiting for the tremors to start before he finally let himself come.

He sprawled out next to me afterwards, in his slacks still but with his shirt off now, and he had me lie on my stomach at his side, so that he could admire the blush of my ass, so that he could place his hand on my burning cheeks and feel the warmth throbbing.

"As long as I can spank your beautiful ass, whenever I want to, whenever I crave," Jack whispered, "I don't care about the rest. Paint the whole damn room red if you'd like. And then I'll whip the same hue into your perfect pale skin."

His words made me tremble as hard as my climax had. His fingers began roaming more purposefully now, up and down, then lower, between my legs, letting me know that he had just started. That the night was still young.

And suddenly I understood. It didn't matter if the rooms were black and white or rainbow-colored, if they were bare or filled to overflowing. All I needed was Jack. He was what made the place home.

About the Author

Called "a trollop with a laptop" by East Bay Express, "a literary siren" by Good Vibrations, and "the mistress of literary erotica" by Violet Blue, **ALISON TYLER** is naughty and she knows it.

Over the past two decades, Ms. Tyler has written more than twenty-five explicit novels, including *Tiffany Twisted, Melt with You,* and *The ESP Affair.* Her novels and short stories have been translated into Japanese, Dutch, German, Italian, Norwegian, Spanish and Greek. When not writing sultry short stories, she edits erotic anthologies, including *Alison's Wonderland, Naughty Fairy Tales from A to Z, Kiss My Ass, Cuffed,* and *Playing with Fire.* She is also the author of several novellas including *Cuffing Kate, Giving In, A Taste of Chi,* and *Those Girls.*

Ms. Tyler is loyal to coffee (black), lipstick (red), and tequila (straight). She has tattoos, but no piercings; a wicked tongue, but a quick smile; and bittersweet memories, but no regrets. She believes it won't rain if she doesn't bring an umbrella, prefers hot and dry to cold and wet, and loves to spout her favorite motto: You can sleep when you're dead. She chooses Led Zeppelin over the Beatles, the Cure over NIN, and the Stones over everyone. Yet although she appreciates good rock, she has a pitiful weakness for eighties hair bands.

In all things important, she remains faithful to her partner of seventeen years, but she still can't choose just one perfume.

An excerpt from

The Delicious Torment

the upcoming second book
in Alison Tyler's Story of Submission series

Prologue

I believe you can fall in love six times before breakfast— that is, if you're looking. If you have an aura of willingness, of curiosity, then others will come find you. Jack understood this intimately, and he worked hard to keep my focus on him. But he needn't have worried. At heart, I'm an extremely monogamous person. I wanted to please Byron. Trust me, I did. Yes, I relished the animosity of our breakup, but only because it was so long coming. For years, I did my best to be exactly the type of girl he wanted. I'm sweet by nature, with a dark edge that rarely comes out. I was always more comfortable being left than leaving.

Yet Jack worried. I could tell. He demanded my constant declarations of submission to him. He wanted me to say, "I'm yours."

I wanted him to say something entirely different, but I bided my time.

Jack and I were both high-strung on desire. On the sofa, we sat with limbs entwined. At dinner, we bent close together, feet touching under the table. We fucked everywhere. *Everywhere.* In his car. In his office. On the beach. In Mann's Chinese Theater. Outside of Griffith Observatory.

I was his. He had to know that. But first he made me prove myself to him—through pain, and shame, and utter humiliation.

And, trust me, shame can be more painful than pain itself.

Chapter One:
Love Me Two Times

I came in the night.

This had happened to me before, but not often. Wet dreams are more rare for women, I think, than for men. But I came. Hard. Picturing Jack using a cane on me, my body bent, knees under my stomach, ass up to receive each blow. The climax was exquisite, and I was covered with a thin sheen of sweat when Jack shook me awake.

"What was that?"

I responded with a sound between a moan and a sigh, lost in my dream.

"Sam, what the fuck was that?"

By now I was slightly more awake, and chilled. Did Jack know what had happened? Could he guess? Normally, a sleep-induced climax might not have been a big deal. But Jack had been working with me, training me to come when he wanted me to come. He'd put me on restriction—this was my second day with no climax—second of a threatened five. That's how greedy I am for pleasure. I couldn't turn off my desires.

My body, subconsciously, had disobeyed him.

Even through the dream haze, some insolent part of me wanted to be flippant. *Earthquake*, I thought to say. But self-preservation kicked in. Instead, pretending to be drowsier than I actually was, I murmured, "What do you mean?"

"You were moaning," he said, and I could hear the dark suspicion in his voice, but he couldn't possibly think I'd made myself come. My wrists were chained over my head, and I was wearing a chastity belt.

"Dreaming," I whispered, feeling sad as the last wisps faded away.

The light flared on, and I heard Jack reaching for the keys. In seconds, I was undone, the cuffs off, the belt off, and Jack's warm fingers had spread apart my nether lips, feeling for the wetness that I knew would prove my guilt.

"You came—" he insisted. "In your sleep. I know the sounds that you make when you climax, Sam. Do you think I'm stupid?"

It was four in the morning. Yet Jack was completely awake. "No, Sir."

"What were you dreaming? Tell me quickly, before you can think of some fancy story."

I sighed and looked away, and Jack gripped my chin and forced me to face him.

"That you were punishing me—"

"How?"

"With your cane..."

"And did I touch you?" The look on his face was intense. I felt as if I were being interrogated at a crime scene, the bright light in my eyes, Jack's unsmiling gaze inches from mine. "Did I fuck you?"

"No, Jack."

"Did you touch yourself?"

"No, Jack."

"You came from the pain alone?"

"Yes, Sir."

"You're not lying to me, are you?" he asked, letting me loose and then leaning back against the pillows, contemplative. He was at ease now. A change had taken place, but I didn't know why.

"No, Sir."

"Describe the dream."

I huddled up under the blankets, arms wrapped around my legs, and I tried to remember all the details. "I was wearing a thin white nightgown."

"Do you own one like it?"

I shook my head.

"Anything like it?"

"A sundress."

"Go get it."

I stumbled from the bed and opened the closet, then pulled a semi-sheer sundress from the rack. I slid the gown over my head, and Jack nodded his approval.

"Continue," he said.

"You told me to get into position."

"What position?"

"Knees bent under me, hands in front of me on the mattress, ass up in the air."

"Show me."

I looked at him, and he moved off the bed, slipping into the black pajama bottoms he'd tossed onto the floor. Jack often started the night wearing the pants, but kicked them off during sleep.

More nervous than ever, I pushed aside the comforter

and assumed the position on the mattress.

"What happened next?"

"You lifted my nightgown, so you could see my ass...."

"Why was I punishing you?"

"I—I don't know."

"Think."

I closed my eyes, and the whole of the dream came back to me. I'd been in a boarding school similar to the one I was creating for my novel. Girls were supposed to wear old-fashioned nightgowns and full-coverage panties to bed, and there had been a nightly check— done by Jack in my dream. When Jack had come to me, he'd discovered that I had left off the panties. A cane had appeared seemingly from nowhere, as Jack had told me to assume the position and had caned me to climax, while the other girls gathered around and watched. Giggling. Pointing.

"Tell me," Jack insisted. "I think you know where we're headed. You don't want to make things worse on yourself."

So I told him. Cast him in the role of headmaster. Explained how I felt when he slowly dragged the fabric up my naked skin, when he revealed my lack of underclothes, when he started to cane me in front of an audience.

"And that made you come," Jack said softly, "that vision."

"Yes, Jack. Yes, Sir."

Jack walked to his cabinet and while my heart started to race, he removed one of his whippet-thin canes. Why couldn't I have come to images of riding on a Ferris wheel or being fucked on a blanket at the beach? Why couldn't I have told Jack that I didn't remember? Jack dragged the dress up, showing off my naked skin. He pressed the cane firmly against me, so I could feel the coolness of the implement, imagine how hot those stripes would be in mere moments.

"How many times did I cane you? How many times before you came?"

It was a dream, I wanted to cry out. *A dream, Jack! How the fuck do I know?*

"Samantha—"

"I don't know, Jack. I just came."

"We'll find out for ourselves then, won't we?"

He started then, before I could think, before I could speak, before I could even breathe. The cane cut into me once, and then almost immediately a second time. He was lining up the blows neatly, orderly, as Jack liked to do. I was still wet from the dream, still swollen from the climax, still lost in the confusing jumbled world of truth and make-believe.

"You'll wear panties to bed or pay the consequences." I felt my breath catch. He was playing. He was taking on a role I'd created. "I'm sick and tired of you breaking the rules. Thinking that sweet little smile of yours will get you out of trouble." And he was changing the script as he went. "I've let you slide before, young lady. From now on you'll feel my wrath each time you cross the line."

The cane slashed through the air, and I cried out, but at the same time, I felt the wetness of my arousal. Felt how turned on I was. Could I come again, solely from being caned and from the way Jack continued to talk to me?

"Were you touching yourself, girl? Is that why you had your knickers off?"

"No, Sir."

"You want me to believe you forgot them?" His voice was mocking.

"I don't know, Sir."

My head swam. Pain and pleasure floored me. And Jack continued playing, clearly enjoying himself.

He kept up a steady monologue as the cane wreaked havoc on my skin. But I felt that climax building within me again, the pleasure managing to overshadow the pain.

"Bad girls are punished under my watch," he continued. "You'll meet me in my office in the morning, for a second dose... One delivered privately, so that we can really get to the bottom of things...."

And that was it. All I needed. My pussy clenching, contracting. Stars in my eyes from holding my breath so long. I shook the bed, as I must have in my sleep, and Jack watched, almost curiously, until I was able to regain my sense of self. He didn't have to tell me what to do. I understood without a word of instruction, lifting my ass back in the air, preparing in case he wasn't finished.

He wasn't, of course. I'd gotten mine. Now he had his.

"Three more," he said, "Count them."

They were the meanest blows yet, the ones with his arm fully behind them, and I was shaking once more by the time he dropped the weapon.

When he was done, he kissed me, softly. He brushed the tears from my eyes, bit gently into my full bottom lip. And then he climbed back onto the bed and pulled me to him, pressing me against his bare chest. His smile surprised me.

"Your dreams are my dreams," he said, then reached across my body and shut off the light.

More from Alison Tyler

Buy 4 books,
Get 1 *FREE**

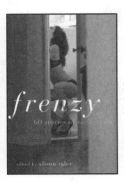

Frenzy
60 Stories of Sudden Sex
Edited by Alison Tyler

"Toss out the roses and box of candies. This isn't a prolonged seduction. This is slammed against the wall in an alleyway sex, and it's all that much hotter for it."
—Erotica Readers & Writers Association
ISBN 978-1-57344-331-9 $14.95

Best Bondage Erotica
Edited by Alison Tyler

Always playful and dangerously explicit, these arresting fantasies grab you, tie you down, and never let you go.
ISBN 978-1-57344-173-5 $15.95

Afternoon Delight
Erotica for Couples
Edited by Alison Tyler

"Alison Tyler evokes a world of heady sensuality where fantasies are fearlessly explored and dreams gloriously realized."
—Barbara Pizio, Executive Editor,
Penthouse Variations
ISBN 978-1-57344-341-8 $14.95

Got a Minute?
60 Second Erotica
Edited by Alison Tyler

"Classy but very, very dirty, this is one of the few very truly indispensable filth anthologies around." —*UK Forum*
ISBN 978-1-57344-404-0 $14.95

Playing with Fire
Taboo Erotica
Edited by Alison Tyler

"Alison Tyler has managed to find the best stories from the best authors, and create a book of fantasies that—if you're lucky enough, or determined enough—just might come true." —Clean Sheets
ISBN 978-1-57344-348-7 $15.95

---

* Free book of equal or lesser value. Shipping and applicable sales tax extra.
Cleis Press • (800) 780-2279 • orders@cleispress.com
www.cleispress.com

Ordering is easy! Call us toll free or fax us to place your MC/VISA order.
You can also mail the order form below with payment to:
Cleis Press, 2246 Sixth St., Berkeley, CA 94710.

ORDER FORM

QTY	TITLE	PRICE

SUBTOTAL _____

SHIPPING _____

SALES TAX _____

TOTAL _____

Add $3.95 postage/handling for the first book ordered and $1.00 for each additional book. Outside North America, please contact us for shipping rates. California residents add 9% sales tax. Payment in U.S. dollars only.

* Free book of equal or lesser value. Shipping and applicable sales tax extra.

**Cleis Press • Phone: (800) 780-2279 • Fax: (510) 845-8001
orders@cleispress.com • www.cleispress.com
You'll find more great books on our website**

Follow us on Twitter @cleispress • Friend/fan us on Facebook